KEEP CALM AND PERFECT YOUR SMOLDER

FLAME SERIES BOOK 2

DANIELLA BRODSKY

DB CO.

ONE

MAGGIE

"SO, who are these people we're eating dinner with again?" Reg looked at Maggie as if this was brand new information he was inquiring after.

She'd told him twice, but he'd been fiddling with his phone while the taxi waited at an endless red light, and she knew he hadn't been listening. She wasn't sure he was listening now, even though he was looking right at her. Later, he'd probably claim she'd never told him their names. There was no point in arguing. He was hopeless at remembering details like names, birthdays, and appointments.

That's why they were running late now. He'd been at the gym, clueless, and she'd been pacing the apartment, trying his mobile with no result. When Reg sauntered in with a podcast turned up so loud her eye began to twitch, he stopped before he'd closed the door to answer a text and hadn't even noticed her standing in front of him with crossed arms.

He jumped when he saw her, and in the process dropped the phone. It landed face up and she garnered some small satisfaction that the touch keyboard had been engaged during the tumble. When he picked it up to check, it had been sent, no doubt with a string of nonsense letters and symbols. *Ha ha.*

"Shit! Maggie! Why are you sneaking up on me like that?"

"Reg. I've been calling you for an hour. We have that dinner with Florence from my work tonight. I put it in our Google calendar and on the calendar on the fridge. We spoke about it on the phone this morning."

"God! I hate calendars! Why do we have to go out on a Friday? It's been such a long week. And you didn't—oh, there, twelve missed calls? A bit much, no? What are they, Kennedys?" He sat on the woven bench and yanked at his shoelaces while she tried not to think how his sweat was going to stain the rattan.

"Please, just get ready, Reg. I've texted them to let them know we're going to be late, but we were meant to be there in ten minutes. It'll take us at least triple that to get to the harbour."

"If we live in Paddington, where the best restaurants in the city are, why are we going all the way to the end of the city?" He pulled his shirt over his head and let it fall on the bench beside him. He put the stinky trainers on top of it and left it like that. The running was slimming him too much. Reg was naturally fit and now he was losing whatever bulk his chest had. And once upon a time, she'd really liked that bulk.

"I will tell you again in the taxi, but for now, please, go shower." Thankfully he made his way down the hall. In front of the laundry room, he stepped out of his pants and kicked them close to but not *in* the hamper.

Maggie bent down to pick them up and recoiled at the soaked nylon.

"*I don't know what to do with myself,*" he started to sing as he fiddled with the shower mixer and steam billowed into the hallway to destroy the sleek hairstyle she'd brushed, ironed, and smoothed into obedience earlier. She recoiled at the sound of the lyrics from his mouth. In her memory, they came from someone else's lips. *Shake it off.*

Maggie tried not to hover over Reg as he slowly futzed with his hair and then pulled on a rumpled shirt; coming from a military family, she did not do rumpled. Looking at him tucking it into the jeans he'd picked up off the floor, with the stain on the knee drove her nuts. She bit her tongue. What would saying, "You'd be putting in more effort for your friends," do except start a fight and make them later than they already were.

They were going to the Sydney Harbour eatery because of the tasting menu. She and Florence were in the food biz. They were on the planning side these days, rather than behind the frying pans, but they both endlessly went on about getting back to their cooking roots. Neither of them had discussed practicalities and, usually, there was wine involved in their oaths to do so, but Monday morning saw them both at their desks, planning and researching, rather than in the trenches.

She wasn't unhappy at Five Dinners, Done!, the meal delivery company taking over Australia, but she wasn't exactly happy either. Except when she spent time with Florence, whom she'd brought on board eighteen months ago. The job had earned an extra star rating after that.

Flo was great company. The best, actually. They'd been promising to do this dinner thing since the week Florence started. They'd been instant friends. And now, here she and Reg were. Rushing, stressing (at least *she* was), but Maggie promised herself she'd calm down in the taxi so she could have a good time with her friend, even if she was feeling ungenerous toward Reg at the moment.

Following what they'd both anticipated would be an excellent couple's dinner, it would be great to take her friendship with Flo to the next level—game nights, weekend trips, the whole group thing. And Florence's boyfriend, Lionel, was meant to be fun and exciting, according to Florence, anyway. Maggie couldn't help thinking his name promised the opposite. *Lionel? What kind of name was that?* Something from a children's book about a wily lion? It stuck in her craw.

He was in the military, so at least they'd have something to talk about. Maggie had grown up in a military family and had worked as a chef at Fort Bliss for five years before she'd emigrated to Australia because of *he who would remain nameless*. But that was a long time ago, and surely she could talk about those times without showing signs of distress.

Reg used a card to pay the cab fare and it took forever. The driver had to reboot his payment system twice. She itched to use the emergency fifty she kept in her purse, but she knew that would piss Reg off. He never carried cash and sorely resented it when she was prepared and he wasn't.

Fine. She'd walk in ahead of him.

The restaurant was in touristville, kitty-corner to the ferry docks, with floor-to-vaulted-ceiling windows overlooking the bridge, the Quay, and the Opera House. As she climbed the stairs two at a time, she peered out the pristine glass to take in the view. It never got old. Sometimes she rode a ferry just for the purpose of appreciating it. The visual was a reassurance—*yes, you got it right coming here.*

Reg would catch up. The glamorous woman at the hostess stand asked for her name. "Maggie Jones," she said. "Table for four. We should have two people here already."

"Yes. You're very lucky. We're not really permitted to seat parties until all the guests have arrived, but *Lionel* was so persuasive, I let them." She shrugged conspiratorially like, *who could resist him, right?* Hostess Barbie clocked Maggie for a response, but what did she know? She'd never met the guy. Her smile, she hoped, masked some of her derision.

Lionel, the Wiley Lion? Maggie hated him already. Which was unfortunate as she'd pictured the four of them renting adjoining cabins on the South Coast and grilling steaks and snorkers over a campfire while the boys one upped each other on barbecue gear—even if Lionel's face was out of focus in the images.

"Let me take you." The woman's cascading blonde waves were picture perfect. They swayed over the back of her miniscule dress as she led.

Maggie looked back, but there was no sign of Reg. Good. Let him sit there for an hour watching the taxi driver reboot the credit card device. If he needed her, he'd ring, surely.

How many nights had she spent listening to his friends drone on about financial jargon she couldn't decipher? The one night she proposed to do something with *her* friend, and he had to go out of his way to ruin it. She wouldn't let him. She believed each person was the master of their own fate.

Still, she tried Reg's phone as she followed the hostess's mesmerizing hairdo around the winding dining room. He didn't answer.

"Maggie!" Florence called, and she got the same punch-in-the-gut gratefulness she always did at the sight of her. Florence waved at her frantically as if she'd been afraid Maggie would never show. She wouldn't sell Reg out, but she wanted to.

Her friend ran to Maggie, her dense corkscrew curls—which she'd let hang loose this evening—blocked the view of their table.

"I'm so glad you're here! They've given us the most amazing *amuse-bouches* while we were waiting! We'll have to get them to bring you one. I cannot wait for you to meet Lionel. Oh, look at me, going on like a teenager! Too much bubbly already, I'm afraid. But, oh well, you'll just have to catch up."

Florence firmly gripped Maggie's arms and smiled like she

couldn't help it. There was a natural kinship impossible to resist–how does she *know me* so well? Maggie often caught herself thinking, even from the first days of their acquaintance–even if Florence was a little more accelerated than the situation warranted. *That's so Flo.* The grin that sprung to Maggie's lips at such an intimate knowledge of her friend was probably just as revealing as Flo's manic welcome. This, finally, was friendship.

Maggie prolonged the hug with one final, meaningful forearm squeeze, Flo's dark hair curtaining her, thankfully, because she felt a tear spring to her eye. God, she loved this girl. Sure, she'd had close friends before, but Flo and Maggie had a chemistry that was effortless and rewarding—a rare combination. Flo seemed to get her as if her whole life had been a study of a person matching Maggie's description, and then she'd found her.

"Come, come," Florence said and pulled her to the table. She could probably write a whole book on the many intimacies Florence had revealed about the man sitting there. Now, finally, she could put a face to the name.

The hostess leaned over their table as if sharing a private joke with said occupant. When she moved away, Maggie saw him. *No.* Her heart kicked. Her chest tightened. *It couldn't be.* He looked a lot like George.

Mother of God, please, don't let it be him. She stumbled on her heel and bent over as if to straighten the shoe while trying to blink the image away, so when she stood, Lionel, Florence's boyfriend, would be at the table, not George. Not the man she'd fallen madly in love with all those years ago at Fort Bliss, and then accepted a spur-of-the-moment invitation from to emigrate to Australia, only to suffer the worst breakup in history. As far away from home as a person could be.

She'd been "seeing" him a lot lately. There was the bus the other day, and a week before, a queue at the supermarket check-out. Surely that was all this was. It hadn't helped to hear Reg singing George's favorite song earlier.

"Sorry," Maggie said, straightening. She shook her hair out, which she'd recently had cut into flippy layers without losing the length. Training her eyes on the table ahead, she saw George. *Fuck. Fuck, fuck, fuck!* Her ankle gave way.

"Need someone to lean on?" Florence said, seeming to have expected such a reaction to her boyfriend. Yes, she remembered too well being on the arm of someone so good looking. Her friend took her elbow, and led her directly to George, who apparently was now Lionel, and introduced him. "Finally, my two favorite people meet!"

George, to his credit, smiled warmly, but gave nothing away. His hair was longer, slightly curly like the way it got in the rain. His skin was tanned as if he'd been surfing every day in his new life. *With Florence. How? How could this be?*

"The infamous Maggie." He stood, smoldering as he always had, and went in for her cheek while she braced herself against the swoon that overtook her—the same reaction as when he had touched her all those years ago, and then, thankfully, embraced her for a moment while she tried to recover. *George! How could Florence's boyfriend—the one she's been waiting to have pop the question—be George? My George?*

When he disentangled himself, he looked into her eyes, and her throat went dry recalling the dream she'd had earlier that week about just that look, followed by one of his erotic kisses. She closed her eyes, an infantile attempt to dislodge the picture from her head. Instantly, the years since they'd been together fell away. *No.* She wouldn't allow that reaction. She couldn't, obviously. Evidenced by the fact that when she opened her eyes he was still there. Smoldering. But now smirking too.

Now was the moment. Own up to it, put it out there. *We*

used to date. Laugh over the awkwardness and then move on. They were all adults.

"Where's Reg?" Florence asked before Maggie could think of anything to say. George/Lionel scanned the room. At that moment, Reg came huffing around that same winding route she'd followed the Mattel hostess along moments prior, when the world still made sense.

Maggie did her best to smile as she palmed in Reg's direction. When he caught her eye, she could tell he was angry. She shouldn't have left him, and she couldn't exactly explain why she had, but now she had bigger problems.

"I've been calling you, Maggie! You didn't tell me which restaurant it was. There were five where we got out of the taxi." He was nearly yelling, which wasn't helping the knee-jerk comparison between Reg and George she was currently cataloguing.

Of course, she'd told him which restaurant. But what was the point to argue that now? Or to remark to herself that George would never have forgotten something like that?

"Florence, Lionel, this is Reg," she said, thankfully without any Freudian slips.

Instinctively, she looked deeply into George's eyes. Somehow, they'd made a silent agreement: they would not tell. It would be too awkward, or hard, or whatever. Forget about being adults. Instead, they would take it to their graves. That would be much better. Now, all she had to do was ignore that smolder.

TWO

GEORGE

THERE WERE things Flo had said about her friend Maggie that made me wonder sometimes, could it be? But I was a man of statistics, averages, odds, and the chances of Flo's friend being my Maggie were slim.

My Maggie was a military chef, not a corporate drone. My Maggie would never like the film, *The Book Club*. It was lame and canned and formulaic, and she had better taste than that. She wouldn't eat sushi for lunch. She didn't like it. In fact, she didn't like fish at all, which was the strangest thing about her.

Sure, in the back of my mind, I knew people could change. But the truth is I didn't *want* my Maggie to change. I wanted her to be frozen in time, exactly as she was, and one day, when we were both in another dimension where everything was perfect, I wanted her to come back to me where she belonged. Those were quiet thoughts, only shed a half-light onto, and so it hadn't seemed to matter whether I allowed myself to entertain the thoughts of Flo's Maggie being my Maggie when it suited. Because my Maggie was a thing of unreality.

But now, here she was. She smelled different. Spicy and deeply sexy. When I leaned in to kiss her, I had to hold back from inhaling her. Her hair was long and moved with her in an incredibly sexy way. God, she looked incredible. The old her was there, but also something new and different. Rather than putting me off like my musings would've had me think, these nuances increased her attractiveness tenfold. There were all the things I'd been crazy for and a whole shedload of new things for me to discover and *become* crazy over. God, I had made a giant mistake letting her go. How had I let so much time go by? I was a moron, that's how.

In the moment, even as I kept my eyes fixed on Maggie, messaging *stay quiet for now*, I knew I was well and truly fucked. I had to have her. And that meant I was going to fuck up at least two lives—and a friendship—in the process. I was a terrible, awful bastard. But this terrible, awful bastard knew that wasn't going to change a thing. I'd let her go once and wasn't about to do it again. She used to say I smoldered when I looked at her. If looking at her was all I was getting to do, I was going to get a lot of practice smoldering tonight.

Reg was in quite a huff. I knew Maggie well enough to know she would have told him which restaurant. She would have put it in a Google calendar that she set up for them to share, and she also would have written it on the U.S. Army calendar she kept on the fridge.

"Women, right?" I said to him, just to stir up the ladies and break some of the tension. I poured the Shiraz Flo had ordered into glasses for Maggie and Reg. "Reggie, should I order you a beer too?"

"*I* will order a beer." This was man stuff. We were marking territory. But Reggie didn't know the half of it. "And it's Reg."

I nodded like I may or may not have been listening to what he said.

The ladies started drooling over the menu, and for a second, I allowed myself to look at Maggie. She was magnetic. Even in her failing attempt to cover up her flustered state. Reggie caught me looking, so I posed a question to her as if I'd only been looking at her while I thought up some polite conversation.

"Flo says you're here for the fish. Like fish, do you?"

"What a strange question, Lionel! Everyone likes fish! Especially chefs! I'm sorry, Maggie! I don't know what's got into him." Flo waved him off.

"Not everyone likes fish," I said. Though it was childish, it felt good to remind Maggie I knew her best.

I knew that look Maggie shot, even if she tried not to aim it at me, and I was instantly taken back half a decade.

If there was anything meaningful in this world, it was remarkable that I met her now, when my whole life was about to change forever.

THREE

MAGGIE

THE DINNER WAS DIVINE, as expected. A kaleidoscope of fresh colors and minimalist plating that rioted in her mouth. But it seemed through each of the degustation courses, the waiter was ready to remove her plate after she'd only managed a bite or two.

George. Was. Sitting. Across from her. He looked even more gorgeous than he did before, if that was humanly possible. Those ridiculous ocean eyes, that magnetic smile. Why was he not a movie star? Because he was also gorgeous on the inside and felt strongly about doing good for the world.

The three years since their parting felt simultaneously like another lifetime and just minutes ago. She tried not to notice the movement of his arms, but she was hyper-conscious of them. In her mind, they were grazing her shoulders while his hands outlined the silhouette of her hips. The more she forced them away, the more intensely they came back. Within moments, she felt like the absolute worst friend and girlfriend in the world. Sure, Reg wasn't on the top of her list at the moment, but he didn't deserve this.

And worse, she was pretty sure George knew exactly what

he was doing to her. She noticed a lack of body connection between him and Flo, and she didn't know if this was normal for them or if she'd done something to bring it on.

Either way, she never felt like more of a terrible, awful person in her life. This was all very wrong. On top of the badness, the ickiness, and the crushing guilt that had buffeted her from all angles as she tried to smile and nod, Maggie felt like there was an elephant sitting on her throat. Despite the giant breaths, she couldn't seem to get in any air. The idea of George in the same restaurant, at the same table, in a relationship with her best friend would not fit into any existing logical framework. And her brain couldn't seem to come up with a new one.

The secrecy appeared to magnify the *George* effect. She guzzled water so quickly, the waiter brought a pitcher for the table; at least he was something for her to look at for a second. But just as she was enjoying the relief of the waiter's capable hands lifting and pouring, even the blessed gift of another few seconds of folding Flo's napkin into an origami hat or possibly a boat, out of the corner of her eye, she saw George smirk. Just as her eyes automatically went to investigate, he made a flash of eye contact with her.

Maggie looked away immediately, shifting to pick up her glass for camouflage, and knocked the whole thing over into the fancy crostini pyramid alongside a truffle butter swipe on a slim slab of marble.

"Oh!" Flo came to the rescue with a de-origami-hatted napkin to dab up the tsunami while the waiter assured Maggie it was absolutely nothing and he'd bring back more Margaret River truffle butter and house-baked *crostino*.

"Crostin*o*?" Reg said under his breath when the waiter retreated. "That's the singular. Someone should really tell him."

"Yes," George/Lionel said. "Can you imagine if he goes around saying that *every night*?"

"You say Crostino, I say Crostini," Maggie said, palms spread.

Maggie had hoped to thaw the ice with her creative lampoon of *Potato, Patah-to*, but she felt George's eyes dart between her and Reg and she knew he didn't approve. She couldn't say her boyfriend's nitpicking didn't annoy the shit out of her too. But she wasn't going to let George know that. She wasn't going to let George know anything.

Now she felt anger swarm into the hive of crazy emotions surrounding her. Why was she so angry?

By the time they'd ordered, clinked glasses to Flo's toast of "friends old and new," and indulged in a ridiculously tasty first course of kingfish ceviche with finger lime and shocking orange fish roe, Maggie was being so profusely bombarded with images of the things she and George used to get up to in private (and sometimes only semi-private) that she had started to see spots.

She excused herself to the *ladies'*, a term which George used to tease her about because she couldn't bring herself to say the word *toilets* to everyone as was the custom here. Her entire body was electrified. She'd forgotten that feeling, the way the whole world faded into a sea of sensation when she was with him.

In fact, the spots she was seeing were only bringing on the memory trip more intensely and at an alarming clip. For a brief second as her hand shoved the bathroom door, her brain sent out the idea that possibly she was dying and hadn't quite made it to heaven. Of course, her afterlife would involve *haute cuisine*, and of course, her realm of unfinished business would star George. *Ridiculous. After all this time!* And yet.

She locked herself inside a cubicle and told herself to calm down. She would not give into tears. Instead, she closed her eyes and tried to concentrate on a thought pattern that might bring her to some proactive action she could take to ease the situation.

Nothing presented itself.

Instead, she was inundated with images of George backing her against the wall of their apartment one night when they promised they would actually keep their clothes on and watch television. There'd been so many nights like it. But she clearly recalled the urgency for him to be inside of her that consistently sabotaged their plans to behave. Hours not only flew when they were together; they rocketed, jumped light years. She remembered moments of wondering where they'd gone, if she'd be forced into some Faustian bargain at some point when reality came knocking. Well, it had knocked and she had felt forced. And miserable. *Shake it off.*

But her brain had its own agenda. She closed her eyes to see them kissing on the stairwell one day when it was pissing-down rain outside, every soaked inch of him pressed against every soaked inch of her. Her abdomen contracted at the memory of his erection against her, the moan he brought to her lips. How many times in the post-George years had she woken terrified that she'd never feel like that again? Reg either didn't know how or couldn't be bothered to bring her to that point.

George had fumbled the keys and they'd both roared with laughter as they clattered to the slippery floor. Once inside, there they were, him pushing aside any barrier so he could slide inside her. The cry of relief as they were once again joined in the most intimate way was a drug to her. She was bold and strong and fearless and could burn the world with her desire if she so chose. But what would she pay in return? This, right here in the toilets, was what she would pay. Oh, she'd known, hadn't she?

The door to the bathroom opened and Maggie was jolted back to the moment. She stiffened, trying to calm her breath, which was making her chest shudder. She felt like she'd been caught.

"Maggie?" It was George.

She didn't say a word. Couldn't. Her body sustained a sudden deep freeze.

"Maggie, I know you're in there. I see your shoes. And your incredible calves. I can only imagine the red toenails you used to have all the time."

"We should have said something," she said.

"I know. But imagine how that would go. This is Maggie, the love of my life, the one who got away. And now she's your best friend!"

"Don't."

"I can't help it. And neither can you." She smelled him. Magnificent. Some understated pheromone thing that made her want to tear down the door with her bare hands.

"I can. And I will." Her own declaration brought her to stand. She could do this. All she had to do was slide the lock, which she did easily enough. But that sent the door between them swinging. And now she saw him, looking and smelling like he did. What she'd been thinking, now, she wasn't so sure. But she *had to be.*

He didn't budge. There was no way past but to touch him. She looked at his arm. He watched her look. She was frozen as if this—making physical contact with no one watching—was the thing that would be the line between good friend and bad.

The second she tried to shoulder through, he caught her arms with his strong hands. "Maggie, don't you think this might be fate catching up with us?"

His lips were so close to hers, she could feel his breath. It took every bit of strength she could muster to shake her head, though that wasn't too far off her purgatory musing. "It's an unfortunate coincidence," she whispered. But her exit from his arms was as slow as molasses. She needed to savor the feeling of his touch because she swore it would be the last time.

Maggie could feel his eyes on her as she washed up at the

sink and walked out the door. Safe on the other side, she finally let out her breath.

"Maggie! There you are!" It was Flo. "I went to the toilets on the other side but didn't see you. I started to worry. Are you okay?"

Did Flo know George was on the other side of that door? Had she heard them? Was he about to walk through? Or was she about to go in?

In an effort to avoid calamity, Maggie squeezed Flo's hand and led her back to the table. "So, what do you think of Reg?" she asked, trying for purchase. Her own world was spinning out of control and she had to slow it down. But one thing was for sure, she didn't have the power to stop it. And the terrible heaviness in her chest as she held the hand of her best friend was only a tiny inkling of the pain to come. That was the other thing she knew for certain.

Everything else? Well, that was in the realm of the unknowable—the magnificent, boundless, unknowable that George had always represented. She'd let herself forget, just a little, how alive she felt in its majesty. But there was no way to forget it now.

"Lionel really likes you. I can tell," Flo said while Maggie avoided eye-contact, pointing to the table as if Flo didn't know where it was.

"Oh?" Maggie pushed off the big swallow she was desperate for.

"Of course! You're Maggie!" And didn't that just say everything and nothing in the most unhelpful way, all at once?

"SO, WHAT DO YOU THINK?" Flo handed Maggie a steaming mug of milky tea and took a seat alongside at her desk.

She was talking about Lionel, who Maggie was trying

desperately not to call George. She needed to keep her cool. Perhaps they could both get through by keeping calm and communicating in a language of silent smolders and everything would be fine. *Sure.* God, his smolder was all she could see. He blotted out the whole world, just the way he always had.

"He's lovely, Flo."

Flo put her face close to Maggie's, noses an inch apart, and stared into her eyes, expressionless.

He'd told her. She was terrified, but also relieved. Maggie was a terrible liar and if this was how she felt after one sleepless night, she could only imagine what weeks of this would be like. Her heart skipped a beat waiting for the angry, hurt words to come tumbling out.

Then Flo's lips curled into a grin and she reached for Maggie's hands, squeezed. "I'm so glad. It was so important to me that you meet! I just had a feeling it would be special."

She hadn't needed to follow George's lead. She could think for herself. But she hadn't seized her chance to be out with it. She'd respected his wishes and she'd felt excessively in the bathroom with him—emotions and physical reactions here, there, and everywhere. And she hadn't been able to stop thinking about him.

There was a good reason he'd decided to omit the truth, she'd thought, because that was how he rolled. But she couldn't think of one that didn't lead to something awful. So, after a weekend of sleepless nights, and a dozen reminders that she'd had plenty of chances since to be out with it, she'd sworn her brain off the topic.

Maggie's control over her thoughts was epic. It was how she'd gotten where she was. Her father had always emphasized the importance of this focus on the present objective in life success, but he needn't have. It came naturally to her.

While Maggie had stared at the ceiling all Friday night after the dinner shock, Reg complained ceaselessly about what a jerk *Lionel* was, calling him *Rog* and such, and she tried to dissuade him, an effort she convinced herself was for the sake of the foursome in which her mind had envisioned them before the meeting. But that wasn't going to happen, was it? How long could she and George, er, Lionel, keep this up? And where would it end? Whenever she tried to think that far, she drew a blank, as if they would all cease to exist. That couldn't be good.

Why had she called George *lovely*? Did that sound bad? Once again, she found herself speechless. It was as if Flo were giving her all these opportunities to make it right and she just hadn't. *Lovely*. Maggie nodded, smiled immensely like she always did when she was lying, which technically she wasn't. But she wasn't going to get by on a technicality here. Because she'd seen and touched and tasted George naked more times than she could count. And even worse, she loved him.

"Not sure he liked Reg very much. But we'll work on it."

Again, Maggie flashed a manic grin.

What had George meant by those words he said? *I can't help it. And neither can you.*

FOUR

GEORGE

OH, it was on. *I can't help it and neither can you.* I shouldn't have said the words out loud, but I had to put it out there. We were meant to be, and there, last night, was physical evidence of the fact. What were the chances of us being brought together that way?

Now that I knew Maggie was living her life so closely parallel to my own, the regular thoughts I'd had of her over the years had become hammering convictions that persistently demanded my attention.

You put the truth out there to Maggie, so what are you going to do about it?

Polite society would dictate I did nothing. But I'd never put too much stock in polite. Where did that get you? Let me do the right thing for the sake of the right thing, even though nobody wins. Pointless. You got one chance to do this life thing, and what would be the point of skipping out on the most important piece?

Say I wanted to be "kind" and I kept my mitts off Maggie because of her friendship with Flo. I'd break up with Flo down the road, both of us angry and resentful for the unnamed tension between us, or I'd stay with her and in doing so, steal the chance for her to have the kind of love she deserved, all while Maggie wound up with some dickhead like Reg, who didn't deserve her, and clearly didn't know how to treat her. Lose, lose.

The funny thing was since I'd returned to Sydney two years ago, I'd gotten used to the sensation of Maggie's memory crouching at the corner of whatever restaurant, bar, beach, or boardwalk I happened to be at.

Sure, I chose to visit the same places we'd spent time together. And in the beginning, I told myself these were just the places I liked to go, the things I liked to do. But I was never fully in the present when Flo and I were there. I wore memories of me and Maggie like a coat and allowed it to enwrap me so that I actually felt like she was with me. I denied it—even to myself. But that is exactly what I was doing.

I hadn't moved on. So why hadn't I gone and got her back? Because I hurt her. Badly. I'd made the wrong decision on every front. Deployed and left her after I took her as far from home as humanly possible. *Great move, dickhead.*

And yet, I was a soldier. And more than that, I was a person of morals unlike my MIA dad, and I followed through on my commitments. I did the right thing, even if it didn't feel right. Did I want to leave Maggie? Fuck no. But was it the right thing to do? I thought so. What we had was incredibly strong, I told myself. It would be fine. Absence makes the heart grow fonder, doesn't it? She knew how much I loved her.

But I was seriously fucking mistaken. The right thing was what Maggie needed. And subconsciously, I figured, hey, she'd done this her whole life. What would one more period of putting aside her personal needs be, if we'd have our entire futures together afterward?

Big error in judgment. Huge. When you find the person who completes you, they are everything you never had before. That's the whole point. And here I was serving up more of the same shit that she'd had to endure all along. Fail. And that's why we weren't together any longer.

THE NEXT TWO weeks were full of dread and remorse. Maggie expected any day that George would break things off with Flo, that her friend would show up to the office puffy-eyed and devastated. Alternatively, she told herself this was crazy and every word he'd said in that fancy restaurant's bathroom were the words of a man who was faced with temptation and had gotten carried away.

She found herself on a rollercoaster of emotions as the days went on and nothing happened. She flip-flopped on which outcome would be worse. She knew which one would be more sexually satisfying. That was a no-brainer. When she wasn't dreading, remorsing, or convinced she was worrying for nothing, she was fantasizing.

That talk in the stalls leading to his palm on the door, her opening the door, locking them inside, kissing passionately, that solid erection in his jeans coming *out* of his jeans. The feel of it on her skin, the squirmy desperation to take him inside her. Sometimes she pictured them at the pub she and Reg frequented, George taking her against the stall wall. Sometimes they ran off together, cue erection leading to similar scenario in a laneway.

She was sick with the whole thing. Her jeans were feeling loose and her bra seemed to hang rather than hug. Food didn't appeal. Except for the smell of bacon, which sent her into a frenzy. *Sex and bacon.* That was their thing. She couldn't help grinning when she remembered.

What was George playing at staying mum? Had she convinced him with her talk in the bathroom that there was no going back? Had he then realized this life he had with Flo was the right one? And if that bothered her the way she was beginning to suspect it did, what the hell was she going to do about that?

He was off-limits. But for someone off-limits, he certainly took up a lot of her time and attention. All of it, basically. And on the other side was an image of Flo, always Flo, looking devastated. The worst part was that as the days passed, she began to see Flo's hurt as a necessary evil, as if it had nothing to do with her. But, of course, it did. She woke suddenly in the night to scold herself. In the mirror, she barely recognized herself.

There were days she could convince herself of a version of events where everything went back to normal. A soulless life with Reg, but a satisfying job, and a wonderful friendship. Especially when Flo came in with such normal domestic squabbles. Lionel had deposited dirty dishes—without even scraping off the food bits—into the sink the seconds after her half hour of washing up and stacking the dishwasher. Stuff like that.

And for a couple of hours, she could believe her own supportive friend act. "Men," she heard herself say. "God, we're all such stereotypes." She could imagine that she had stopped thinking of George in a way that she shouldn't be.

But then she did. It would start innocently, trying to recall George's relationship with dishes when they'd cohabitated. Had he been pulling out all the stops for her, because she could recall many occasions when she'd made him a beautiful dinner and then he'd filled her wine glass and gently nudged her out of the kitchen while he did the washing up. Sometimes without a shirt, because she was once being cheeky and told him how much of a turn-on that was.

He had his own method for cleaning, which regretfully didn't involve rinsing the soap too carefully from the dishes, but she never felt bothered by that. Little things like that never bothered her with George the way they did with Reg. She remembered sneaking peeks at George while his muscles flexed in a sponge grip. She recalled jokes about "liking his foreplay," and she recalled more than once, the foreplay quickly turning to the main act, the aforementioned bubbles popping on her bare skin, his hands in all the right places as he wedged himself into her on the benchtop.

On one bus ride home, she closed her eyes and was instantly back to their first night together. Well, it was more like their first morning together, and she had congratulated herself when she woke to realize she still had her clothes on. Because she'd sworn she wouldn't sleep with him the first night.

It had been a whirlwind. He'd taken her to a new Spanish restaurant near Fort Bliss she'd been meaning to try. The chef had graduated the year before her at the same Providence, Rhode Island, culinary school, and she'd always been in awe of him.

It was so funny he'd wound up right here in Texas, but his wife was from a military family and this is where she wanted to live. It was very romantic. They'd come to their table with some special *amuse-bouches*, and the chef had introduced his wife with an intoxicated love so palpable, it left a texture over their first date.

Maggie had that blissful lens as she looked around the

Catalan eatery's minimalist interior with its subtle geometric motifs, low lighting from blue pendants shining spotlights on the tables, because she felt like it was a place of love. In her memory, it still was.

She wouldn't have said that out loud on a first date, but the Tempranillo had gone to her head, and there was something about George that made her talk too much. It wasn't that she was nervous. It was more like wanting him to know every single thing about her, down to the thoughts in her head—like this was an essential requirement to her existence. She raised a palm to her mouth. "Sorry. I don't know why I said that. I didn't mean our love. I just meant—"

He cut her off, pulled her hand into both of his and held it there. "I know exactly what you mean."

And she was sure he did. It was an incredible evening, where everything was right.

Slow down, she kept telling herself.

But she hadn't been capable. On that first night, she'd told him about how she felt the day Jessica had married her dad, the terrible pain and surrealism of standing alongside them at the altar, hyper-aware of the red hair she'd inherited from her mother, picturing the texture of her mother's red-headed corpse under the ground, the hair supposedly so slow to fall out. It was a grotesque vision for a first date.

Everything she did should have turned him off. But it couldn't. She was sure of that. There was a current between them, and the time spent in proximity—closer and closer until his hand was on her thigh and hers under the hem of his shirt—only cranked it up. By the time they left the restaurant, he'd guided her by the hand down the block, each squeeze of her fingers in his grip pulsing at her core.

He stepped her inside a crowded bar, the sound system staticky, the song vaguely familiar. As he led her through the sea of people, she was barely aware of where they were going. It was difficult to see past him, and there didn't seem to be a point. She'd never felt such a heightened reaction to anything or anyone.

She'd never let herself, sure, but she'd also never seen a glimmer of anything resembling this. But it was like that old saying, you'll only suffer until the hurt is worse than the cure. And if George was the cure, she was a very, very lucky girl.

By some miracle, he spotted a vacant sofa and they sat. Within seconds, they were all over each other. Holding off sex that first night had been no small feat. In her mind, she felt that if she could at least do that, here was some solid ground she could cling to, despite how slick her body was.

But the next day, she wasn't so lucky. In his tee shirt and her tiny panties, she was standing before his stovetop frying bacon—she liked to cook it low and slow to get it just right. He came up behind her in his tiny soldier's accommodation kitchen and the rest was sex and bacon history.

She felt him solid, just a hint, then a gentle nudge, then a wonderful pressure. Her eyes closed, her head fell back into the crook of his neck, her ass thrust back into him. His hands explored under the tee shirt, hiking it up so he could feel her hip, her ribs, her nipples, the mounds of her breasts.

She wanted him all over her. As he kissed her ear and neck, she lost herself in the sensation. She could hear the bacon pop, felt a hot burst of oil on her exposed belly, and that's when she cried out and hit the point of no return.

Encouraged, George slipped his hand inside the front of her panties, teasing at the trim patch, gently easing her apart with his finger.

"You are so wet," he said and dipped two fingers inside her.

"It's you. I need you. I have to have you now, even though I should wait."

"Oh, you should not wait. You need this. I need this." He lowered his shorts and she felt the bare length of his cock on her ass.

"Yes," she moaned. "Yes. I need you inside me. Please, don't make me wait."

"And just think, I prepared a whole bunch of counter arguments."

She laughed, fully, deeply.

The gales were brought to a breathtaking stop as he pulled her panties aside at the crotch and teased her with his tip. She was molten at their contact. Her body froze, her breath caught. And then he thrust into her.

"Oh God," she cried as he moaned, his rhythm a natural match for her own, a delirium taking hold of them. Every bit of her lit up. He leaned her deeper over the counter, the bacon sizzling loudly now, a hand at her back. She longed to pull his fingers around her tighter, as if to say, I'm yours, I'm yours. She wanted him to make his mark, do what he needed in order to formalize the connection. It was terrifying and wonderful and beyond her comprehension.

His thrusts came faster, then he slowed himself in an effort, she was sure, to keep riding the edge they were both teetering on. He slid all the way out, then all the way in. Again, and again.

"Fuck!" she said.

"Oh yeah, that's it," he called out, now tightening his grip on her neck as she'd willed him to do. His pace quickened. She pushed back against him, lost in animal instinct in him, and then her eyes squeezed shut as her body tightened in great pulses around him, sending him to come too. They stood like that, his arms tightly around her.

"I—" was all he said.

When he pulled out and she felt him release, hot and wet on her thighs, she turned and he kissed her again and again.

Suddenly, he stopped. "Bacon's ready," he said, feeding her a too-hot, oily piece, which she gobbled down hungrily.

"I like sex and bacon," she said, unbeknownst to her immortalizing the saying between them.

That was a Sunday. They'd both called in sick the next three days.

NOW, every moment she spent in the office, she felt more duplicitous than ever. Here was Flo thinking everything was normal while Maggie knew their relationship was on a timer, punctuated by her lewd fantasies playing out sometimes with Flo only feet away.

Even worse, more than once she'd brought herself to orgasm the second she walked into her apartment—first after that bus ride, thinking about him, running out to buy bacon for dinner, and finding herself getting wet just from the scent. Then just from the thought of the scent, like Pavlov's dog. Soon it was a daily habit. She half hoped Reg would find her that way, her hand down her knickers, to start the conversation.

She was going nowhere. Fast.

She found herself frequenting their old shared haunts—Bronte, Coogee, the pub across from their old place, in the hopes he was also in that headspace. But so far, nothing.

At home last week, Reg had made her an elaborate, if inedible dinner of roasted chicken with some fancy sauce that didn't quite come together as it did in the photo he showed her when he'd mentioned the romantic dinner he was going to make for her. But within a couple of days after the baconless chicken, he seemed to be as absent and inattentive as ever. His nose in his phone, his butt denting the sofa cushion on the far end from where she sat.

At least that she could talk to Flo about honestly, so they seemed to be spending a lot of time on the topic of Reg.

"You're too good for him," Flo advised. "These are the kinds of problems people have after ten years of marriage, not in the honeymoon phase."

Flo was right. And she seemed to genuinely care. But she also seemed to have an insight that scared the crap out of Maggie.

After a couple hours talking with her, Maggie found herself once again on the bus to Bronte, walking the old trail to Coogee she'd worn out with George, hand-in-hand. Then jumping in to swim the waters they'd splashed in together like she was just exercising, instead of reliving a time when there was still a chance for the two of them.

Perhaps George had gone away for work and that's why she hadn't heard anything. This was her latest theory on the state of play. But she was too uncomfortable asking whether George was away, and Flo hadn't offered up any conclusive information.

Maggie had always driven and picked George up from the airport, though he tried to talk her out of it. She used to pack him little notes in his suitcase, so he'd think of her while he was away. She'd have a cold beer waiting for him in a mini esky. They could barely wait to get out of the car before their clothes were off. Sometimes they couldn't.

She could text him to find out what, if anything, had happened since the bathroom powwow, but what if Flo saw her number on his phone? What if she already had? And if he'd chosen to agree with Maggie, to forget the whole thing, and he was trying to go about his life with Flo, was it right to push anyway?

As the days slouched past, she felt immersed more than ever

in two distinct lives: the tangled web of the present, and her past with George—sitting at their favorite cafe with its riches of gleaming baked goods, pushing through the hard ocean laps when exhaustion threatened to stop her, lying on a towel after she'd overcome exhaustion, invincible with visions of George and the sun's rays to warm her skin at the corner of the beach alongside the rocky pier where they'd always lain together. Only now, she was actually there alone, in a limbo life that didn't address either reality. Tomorrow. Tomorrow she'd do something about it.

SIX

GEORGE

I SAW her at our spot. Why hadn't I told Flo yet? More than anything, I wanted to walk up to Maggie, throw my arms around her bare shoulders, and let the world think what it might.

I walked down to Coogee and drank a beer at the pub across the way while I watched Maggie sit in our old spot on the sand. It was where all the beautiful women went topless. The first time I showed her, she said, "Oh, they're going to get sunburnt!" indicating the perfect tits on a blonde soaking up the sun.

I said, "You know what? You're right. I'd better go over there and help her out." I started to stand, and she pulled me down. We kissed and laughed and kissed and probably fondled each other a bit much for a public beach. It was one of my favorite memories.

I told myself she was sitting there now reliving the same old times as me, that she wanted a second chance at them too. And I thought how it was my fault we weren't actually soaking up that patch of sun together. She sat up, untied the strings of her bikini top and turned over on her stomach, resting her head on crossed arms. Oh god, what I would give to be that towel.

I thought of how I'd wound up with Flo instead of Maggie. I

hadn't actually asked Flo to move in, but she'd been homeless suddenly, all of which seemed vaguely sketchy at the time and now struck me as doubly so. Why had I been so lackadaisical about such a huge step? Because it hadn't seemed to matter much either way, probably.

Soon after that, she began studying at William Blue's culinary program. It was hospitality this and hospitality that. There was genuine excitement, and it was so different from her executive assistant past that she seemed to be experiencing the world in a whole new way. And all the talk about food reminded me of Maggie, in a good way. I'd loved her giant meals, being her recipe guinea pig, and Flo's new food culture was a way to reminisce.

While she studied, Flo was only working part time and didn't have a huge income, so I didn't feel it was right to break things off during her study, so I stuck with her, though I began to clearly see the fissures in our relationship. There was nothing *wrong* with Flo. She was beautiful, vivacious, intelligent. What was it? I asked myself over and over because in theory, our lives were pretty great—nice place, good friends, fun holidays—what was holding me back from falling in love with Flo?

And then she came home one night, soon after she'd secured the position at *Five Dinners, Done!* mentioning a coworker named Maggie. *That's what's holding you back, mate. She's not Maggie.*

Each time Flo spoke about Maggie, I began to allow myself to imagine it was the real Maggie, my Maggie. I pictured them, heads bent over those enormous menu sheets Flo brought home, and it felt strange, but also wonderful. Maggie was back in my life. And Flo had brought her there.

Now, here was the actual Maggie sitting on this beach thinking of me; she must be. Why else this spot, those revealed breasts? I picked up my drinking pace, downing three pints on the pub's veranda while she lay there, looking around. She'd see me, wouldn't she? And if she did, then what?

I told myself this was our mutually-agreed-upon way of being together for now. She shaded her eyes and looked straight ahead once, but if she saw me, she didn't let on. An hour later, my jeans feeling snug, I watched her dress, look around—for me?—and then make her way up to the winding path toward the main drag.

Letting her go that evening in the sherbet-streaked sunset was the hardest thing I've ever done. But I promised to do this right. And I was a man of my word. I hurt her badly and sensed she blamed some weakness in herself for our breakup. If I was going to do this, then I was going to do it right. That would make the doing all the sweeter, wouldn't it?

Even so, I gave myself one last loophole. I told myself that if Maggie turned and saw me, then we'd have this time together— if she'd let us. But she didn't. It took every ounce of self-control to watch her go because this time Flo wasn't here to stop me.

SEVEN

GEORGE

GEORGE: Can't stop thinking about you. One rainy day in particular in mind. There's this spot on your neck, where you've got a tiny freckle, and every time I picture it I—

"George, what are you looking at on that phone? You look downright devilish," Flo asked from her perch on the sofa. I was at the breakfast bar across the open-plan unit. I was such an asshole. I went to poke at the backspace button and pressed SEND instead.

Great job, George. Put all your cards on the table before the game even began. If this was my chance to make things right with Maggie, I sure as hell wasn't off to a great start.

Still, there was something to be said about being upfront this time around. It was the assumptions that had got us here in the first place. Sure, I'd done the right thing, I was telling myself, when I saw the swirling dots. Maggie was responding.

The dots disappeared.

Started up again.

Disappeared.

I checked my phone more times than I'd like to say, but she didn't text back. Not that day and not the next.

By close of business, I was shutting down my computer and gathering my things when my phone pinged a message from my backpack. It was true: a watched pot never boils.

MAGGIE: I have spent enough time to send me on a one-way ticket to hell imagining how you might finish that sentence.

My response was out before I could think about it.

Well, maybe I can show you.

MAGGIE: No!

GEORGE: No?

MAGGIE: No.

MAGGIE: But . . . maybe if you only tell me it isn't so bad.

EIGHT

MAGGIE

SHE DIDN'T KNOW what she was thinking. No, she did. But the logic was severely fractured. She figured if they released the pent up sexual tension building up over the past four years, and most pressingly, over the last two weeks, via text message, *sexting*, she knew it was called, which felt silly, but seemed to back up her theory (i.e., *not* sex), then they'd be done with it and could move on. Healthy! Modern! Genius!

She even began to feel euphoric, like she'd stumbled upon the perfect solution and was on the brink of enlightenment, which should have been a hint at how ridiculous the strategy was. But she was desperate.

Maggie got through these days by splitting her life in two. The upstanding part knew that if she tugged at that thread, nothing good would come of it. This Maggie went to work, brushed *and* flossed, and ate healthy meals. She exercised according to a detailed schedule and ticked off items on her to-do list like a saint.

But she wasn't fooling herself.

Because the other Maggie had taken to sexting her best friend's boyfriend like a fiend.

GEORGE: What are you wearing?

She was wearing her tatty workout gear because she'd just returned from an hour on the treadmill. An hour! She'd never run a full hour before. And it had gone by in a snap because she'd been mulling over what he said he wanted to do when he thought about that spot on her neck.

GEORGE: Every time I think of that spot on your neck, I'm right back on that rainy day, behind you, stupidly turned on. I start thinking about the desire to press my lips to your skin, and the way I'd lose myself when I made contact, that little moan you used to make . . . and I haven't thought about anything since.

MAGGIE: I remember what you felt like behind me.

GEORGE: Oh, what are you doing to me Maggie?

MAGGIE: There's no answer to that. It's just the way it is. This is just the way it is between us.

GEORGE: Always was.

She had to change tracks because they'd get into all the serious stuff on this path, and that's not what this was about. This was a safe space for the alternate sliding doors version of them—unfettered by emotional baggage, pure desire in action.

MAGGIE: And then you pressed into me.

GEORGE: Oh, you've gone there.

MAGGIE: Can't help it.

GEORGE: Oh Maggie.

SHE TOOK A BREAK AFTER THAT. It was heating up too fast. But she shouldn't have been surprised. That's the way it had always been with them.

And now here he was again, asking what she was wearing. Well, she wasn't a liar.

"Having a shower!" she yelled to Reg, who was wrapped up

in some strain of football she couldn't quite identify. He grunted an acknowledgment.

Her body felt taught and deliciously fatigued from all the exercise. Every bit of her was alert, as if bits of her had finally set off their ON buttons. She felt superhuman. She remembered this feeling. And how addictive it was.

Even the bubbles slid down her body bubblier than before. When she reached her center of gravity, *oh yes*, that bit was definitely getting into the mood. Who would have thought sexting could be so sexy?

Let's face it. Sexting with George *is this sexy.*

By the time she toweled off and took in her curves in the mirror, Maggie was off-the-charts turned on. She knew exactly what she would wear to answer his question.

There was a whole drawer dedicated to lingerie, but it had been so long since she'd worn it, Maggie had forgotten the strap on that particular bodysuit was too long. The black silk strap kept slipping off her shoulder. She checked herself out from behind, over her shoulder in the closet's full-length mirror and realized the effect was perfect. The strap slipping off her shoulder worked.

She held up the phone and clicked a close-up of her shoulder. Tasteful, but a serious taste. Before she could think, she thumbed SEND.

George's response was immediate.

More please.

Again she held up the phone, this time zooming out to show the bare shoulder in the context of her black lace-covered back and the top curve of her ass.

SEND.

GEORGE: Is a staff meeting the right place to be hard for you? No. But right now being bad feels good.

MAGGIE: And there's more.

GEORGE: The CDF is right across the table.

Oh, the Chief of the Defence Force would love this, she thought, clicking a full body shot, bent over her dresser.

Just as she tapped the red circle to capture the shot, she saw Reg enter the room in the corner of her phone camera. Her chest went cold and her breath stopped suddenly.

"What in the world are you doing?" he asked.

She was trying to come up with something seductive, a lie. But dishonesty did not come easily to her. Thankfully, Reg beat her to the punch.

"I'm not in the mood, Dearest."

Maggie wasn't sure what was worse: that he could see her like this and have no reaction, or that he'd taken to calling her *Dearest.*

WORSE STILL: she saw him as a mere momentary roadblock to her X-rated texting with George. What was she doing here? Rushing was not something that came naturally to her. But she'd been in this three-year relationship thirty-five months too long.

When Reg walked out and closed the door behind him, she found she was relieved and picked up where she left off.

GEORGE: I don't care if I get fired. I need you to tell me what you would do right now if you could.

Not do *to me,* but *do.* It was never just about him. It was—is, if she was being honest—the sum of them together that produced the indescribable feels.

MAGGIE: Well. You're better off asking what I wouldn't do.

GEORGE: If we're going off history, not much.

MAGGIE:

GEORGE: History's all we have. DELETE. There were some incredible times. Still could be.

MAGGIE: Does this actually count as sexting? Feels like dangerous territory.

GEORGE: As long as it's got text involved it's fair play.

MAGGIE: I like your justice system.

GEORGE: Thought you might.

Should she rachet things up on the heat index the way he was suggesting? She certainly felt desperate for him, but it felt a bridge too far. Teasing was one thing, getting off together something quite different.

While she debated the scales of justice, the texting dots began to swirl.

GEORGE: Well, if you're going to make me wait, I'm going to take the lead.

More dots. She was soaked and hitting the bursting point. Where did that fit in on the justice scales?

GEORGE: I'd slide up behind you.

Just what she'd been picturing.

GEORGE: Press in. Feel you shudder—my favorite part, by the way, then run my lips and tongue all over that spot on your neck, all while you pushed back into my cock.

There. He'd said the word. She was trembling, picturing him, looking at herself, feeling herself riding the edge of everything. Maggie's hand slipped down toward her wetness.

GEORGE: Shit, gotta go.

And then he was gone.

Maggie fell back on her bed and squeezed her eyes shut. *I will not meet up with him. I will not meet up with him.*

Two hours later, she was *not* sleeping next to Reg when George finally texted back.

GEORGE: Sorry about that. National security or some crap not as important as where we were.

I MISS YOU is what she wanted to type.

MAGGIE: It was a beautiful fantasy.

GEORGE: *It's more than that. You'll see. Goodnight for now. xx*

Their first kiss. What in the fuck was she falling into?

WAS it bad getting hard in a meeting with the CDF and the whole team about why I was chosen for this deployment and what an honor it was meant to be? Sure. Did it feel good? Maybe even better for the taboo factor? Of course.

And the symbolism of my work versus Maggie certainly wasn't lost on me. It was like we kept trying to keep it light and naughty, but reality wanted us to remember there were other layers to this.

When the base went into lockdown for the first time in my experience and I couldn't get inside to work, well, that should have run a cold shower over the whole thing. But all that happened was that I walked along Oxford Street trying not to get on a bus to find her and tear her clothes off.

The lockdown was the perfect chance. I was meant to get a text when we could get back on base, but after half an hour when I hadn't heard anything, I realized I'd passed the pizza shop and the burger joint and I was walking straight to her apartment. What did I think I was going to do? Knock on the door, ask Reg if I could borrow his girlfriend for a while, then close us in the bedroom and do all the things running at mad pace through my head?

Of course not.

So why was I still walking?

Because you miss her, fuckwit.

It was dark by the time I got to her place, like a madman, doing the one thing I kept telling myself not to do.

I counted the windows to her third-floor unit. Three floors, she probably got sick of climbing stairs. I pictured her at a beautiful cottage in Coogee, like the ones we'd dreamed about in her first days here, overlooking the sea. One floor, just the two of us, cozy. Maybe it wasn't as crazy as it sounded.

All the windows of her flat were dark. I could tell which one opened to their bedroom because the unit beneath had its lights on and a man who should have been wearing more clothes wasn't, as he was sprawled on his bed with the shades and windows wide open.

Sorry about that. National security or some crap not as important as where we were.

I tapped SEND and immediately saw a light, which must have been her phone. The light moved. She was reading it. Had she been waiting for it? What would she do if she knew I was right outside her window?

I saw the shadow flicker inside her room as the dots swirled on my phone, foretelling her reply. The thought of her fingers, her hands, her body, overwhelmed me. I could feel the motion of her thoughts and words bringing us toward the future . . . together.

It was a beautiful fantasy.

No. It couldn't be only that. I couldn't live in a world with a reality of that shape.

It's more than that. You'll see. Goodnight for now. xx

I walked home. A man with a plan. Step one: talk to Flo. This had to end.

TEN

MAGGIE

MAGGIE: Please don't tell Flo. I have the strongest feeling you're about to, but I can't hurt her this way. In fact, the sexting has to stop too.

The text had been a meagre way of *doing something* after Flo had come into the office in tears.

"I think Lionel's cheating on me," she'd said.

Maggie nearly lost her breakfast, fessing up then and there. As it was, a fair amount of tea came out of her nose.

"Why?" she asked.

"He's been glued to his phone, and when he's not on his phone, he isn't home. Something's going on."

Maggie opened her mouth to tell the truth, but her body resisted. *What good will come of it?* What was this her gut was saying? *You can't be with him. Remember how it turned out? You're still a wreck from that. You're having a bit of fun, but even that keeps dipping into serious territory. No point in hurting Flo. Things cannot happen between you.*

And she found crisscrossing the moral ground less difficult than she'd expected. *Everyone lies,* she told herself. *Especially when it comes to cheating, everyone knows the confessions only serve to ease the conscience of the cheater. A purely self-serving act.*

And picturing Flo's beautiful, child-like eyes bugging at the revelation of their deception only supported her theory. It would be horrendous.

There, she thought, after the text to George. *Better.* But she didn't feel better. And why hadn't he answered? Had he already said something? At lunchtime, Maggie walked in the blazing sun to her favorite florist to buy a fabulous undone bouquet for Flo, full of gum leaves and alien yellow fluff balls that looked too beautiful to occur naturally.

But on the way home, she worried the gesture made her look guilty. Sure, she should feel bad for her friend who worried her boyfriend was cheating, but was buying flowers too much? Did they scream, *It's me! He's sexting with me!* Maggie hated the idea of orchestrating her friendship, the only one that had ever naturally got on like a house on fire.

At an overflowing bin, the hand holding the bouquet (a *posy* they'd call it here) hovered. In the end, she decided to present it to Flo. Surely doing something was better than doing nothing.

"Oh, Maggie! So thoughtful, thank you." She rushed into the kitchen to find an empty vase and then let the flowers fan out in their fresh water. "So much beauty," Flo said, shaking out her curls at the back the way she did a dozen or so times a day, "makes me think maybe things aren't as ugly as I think."

Maggie returned to her desk heavy-hearted. The message, the flowers, even the moral prevarication—none of it offered relief.

She'd purposely left her phone at her desk when she'd presented the flowers to Flo. Another deception. But there hadn't been any reason to worry. George hadn't texted or called. Even if only for a second, the idea flashed: could she tell him to forget the forgetting about telling Flo?

. . .

THAT AFTERNOON, a bomb dropped. Partners were now not only invited, but encouraged, to attend the conference in Noosa, a beautiful resort town on Queensland's Sunshine Coast. The company was looking to expand, and some potential investors were coming to a few of the social events there. They needed to broadcast shiny happy people to rack up the zeros on the investment front.

The kibosh was probably for the best, then. Otherwise, how would they get through a weekend of sexting with the happy foursome in the same room? She could, what, simply pretend they were two people recently introduced at a dinner by Flo. *Sure. That could happen.*

Aside from the George bomb, it occurred to her that there was something not quite right about her apprehension around Reg spending the weekend in Noosa with her and her work colleagues. These days, they were more like two people existing alongside each other than anything resembling a couple. And she hated to think how obvious that would be. Perhaps she was looking at this the wrong way, though. Could this be a chance for them to rekindle? Swear off George and see if she could give Reg the old college try?

Still, for something to rekindle, there needed to be kindling, and she wasn't sure there was. She sensed her increase in derision toward Reg had something to do with the comparison of him side-by-side to George. (She'd given up trying to think of him as Lionel.) The conference could be a test of sorts, give it her all and see if sparks could ignite. A voice inside shouted, *Sure! Combustible conditions are perfect for sparks!* But not the kind she was after.

And how was that Reg-sparking going to work with George lasering her with those looks like he had at the dinner? With the illicit photos she'd messaged him? Her pledge to do the right thing seemed so quaint and naive now. How had she ever imagined she'd stick to it? And what was all this self-delusion she was tossing up now? She was checking her phone for texts from George and not actually looking at the time, and she knew it.

She was a terrible, awful human who deserved whatever was coming her way, because it *was* coming. There was no doubt about that.

Her phone pinged. Maggie ignored it for a good thirty seconds like that was some great achievement.

GEORGE: I will wait for direction from you, if that's what you wish. I don't want to make this any more uncomfortable for you or Flo than it already will be.

Instead of relief, she had opened a new can of worms. *What is* this? she wanted to type. But she knew how that sounded. These were not questions to be asked so early in such a giant cluster-fuck. Especially when she was trying to resist anything happening.

MAGGIE: Thank you.

GEORGE: BTW I'll be coming along to Noosa. I'm hoping I can keep on my best behavior.

She began typing, *you'd better!* When he beat her to the punch with: *But I think we both know that's not going to happen.*

George, was all she could think to say. And whatever sentiment he drew from that, he evidently didn't feel the need to respond.

She was going straight to hell.

Whether in an effort to detract attention from her guilty bouquet shenanigans, or because she needed her friend, or wanted her friend to benefit from the misery loves company effect, Maggie shared the rekindling plans she had for Reg at the conference.

They were in the break room, and both were waiting for a pot of proper T2 Melbourne Breakfast tea to brew. (Benefit of working at a culinary outfit.) I'm going to miss this, she thought as she'd pulled out the mugs and scooped the tea leaves into the minimalist pot. The routine of their friendship was as warm-fuzzy inducing as the friendship itself. Except, already it wasn't. Here she was, overthinking, overcompensating, clunking around the space formerly known as warm-fuzzy.

Her friend made the perfect lewd jokes, eyebrow raises, and rested a comforting hand on Maggie's shoulders as if to highlight how simple this friendship would be if only Maggie wasn't secretly in love with George.

Thank God for Flo was something she'd thought more times than she could remember, and that was why she should resist any temptation where George was concerned, despite the constant loop of his words and the already over-the-line sexting: *The love of my life, the one who got away. I can't help it, and neither can you.* How dare he say those things to her.

That's what she should text George. But she didn't. Instead she left it at them both knowing they weren't going to be on their best behavior. And found herself grinning about it more than once.

"And what are *you* thinking about?" Flo said, pouring Maggie's tea through the strainer. And there she'd been caught thinking about it again. Following the talk of the lingerie, waxing, and seduction of Reg plans, hopefully she hadn't given anything away. Still, she felt caught. Which she was getting used to.

Maggie shrugged and excused herself back to her desk, where she found herself questioning the power of her mental kibosh. While she needed to rely on it, she found herself instead daydreaming about George thinking of her red toenails, gazing hungrily at the image of her lingerie laden backside. He could be doing that right now for all she knew! She typed out texts and then deleted them.

But the very last night before the trip, she couldn't make herself delete one: *Thinking of you looking at that photo of me.* This was the problem with instant communication. There were only so many times you could control yourself.

Is there a hidden camera in here? Would be pretty hot if there were.

And with that, they were back on the sexting. And before she knew it, she was on a plane, trying not to look two rows behind her where Flo and "Lionel" sat.

MAGGIE HAD GONE whole hog in preparation for the *last chance with Reg* bit of the trip: bikini wax, fresh haircut, and eyebrow shaping. When her hairstylist had commented how long it had been since she'd seen her, Maggie realized she'd been slack in the self-care department for a while now. She was doing it for Reg, she told herself, really giving this holiday the full chance it deserved. She'd packed skimpy, smutty lingerie—the kind he liked more than she did. *There,* she told herself, *that proves I'm not doing it for George.*

At the last minute, she added one more item to her suitcase: would it be so bad if she also packed the little black lacy number she'd worn for George's photo? *It turned her on* was her thinking, and what was the difference how she got there?

Yes. She heard herself. But denial was a powerful thing.

By any visual scorecard, Maggie was certainly ticking all the relationship-saving boxes. Organized as usual, she'd even sat down to memorize a list of conversation topics. She looked over to see Reg browsing the in-flight magazine. Perfect, she was set to talk about a few new restaurants in Noosa. Local dining was number two on her list. Reg let out a huge yawn then patted his mouth.

Late night? She wanted to ask. He'd stayed up watching a game hours after she'd gone to bed. But she didn't want to be provocative, so thankfully, she was prepared with number two. "Anything in there about that new seafood spot, Conkers?"

"Yeah. Just saw that one. Get the chili mud crabs, it said."

"Cool." Her mind blanked after that one word. And stayed blank. Why couldn't she think of anything to say? She had a list. *You shouldn't need a list to talk to your boyfriend.*

"Chili mud crabs," he repeated, like he, too, had nothing to say. How had this happened to them? What did they used to talk about? All of a sudden, the idea of strapping on that lingerie, all that grunting and groaning, putting in the endless time it took for him to finish, seemed exhausting. Could all this effort manufacture the desire she was looking for? The desire she never needed to manufacture for George. Maggie yanked at the collar of her shirt which instantly felt constricting.

She would give it her all. There was no way she was ending this relationship without knowing she'd gone out fighting. Desire or not, she was going to get sexy with Reg, no matter what it took. And if that failed, she certainly wasn't letting the ending have anything to do with George.

She *could* help it. No matter that the intense tingle along every inch of her skin was merely a result of thinking the G word. No matter the sexts. No matter her mouth had betrayed her and hinted at their sexual past in the Qantas airline lounge. *Bacon.* She had to go and say that, after all the planning, all the steeling herself for being impenetrable to his um, penetration. They hadn't even boarded the plane and there she'd been putting images in his head of their sultry mornings of sex and bacon. Oh, he wouldn't have missed the reference. And though she wasn't purposely looking, she did see how hard he'd instantly gotten at the sound of the words.

Now what would George be thinking two rows back? He would have figured she had changed her mind, that she was going to give into her feelings, and what? They'd be at this hotel snogging in dark corners, partners be damned? Oh, this was not good. This was the opposite of good.

Whenever Maggie felt her head turning to get a look at him a few rows back, she pinched the inside of her wrist. Still, one time, right before landing, she didn't pinch quite hard enough. And of course he caught her. That knowing smile. He was so onto her. This was going to be a long couple of days.

ELEVEN

GEORGE

A FEW DAYS in Noosa would be great for my libido, terrible for my promise to Maggie, I'd told myself when I agreed to go with Flo to the conference. Normally, I made decisions in a matter of minutes and this was no different. I'd been trained up on this at Duntroon's officer course, and then tested in real life scenarios throughout my career. Lives depended on it in the military and they depended on it here too.

I listed out the risks, the possible outcomes, the ways everything could turn to shit, what to do in each eventuality, and got everything in place for all the worst-case scenarios. This decision traced out to a lot of worst-case scenarios. But the worst worst-case would be squandering this chance to spend time with Maggie. And we were off to quite a bacon-sizzling start.

When I caught Maggie looking at me down the plane aisle, I could see how pissed she was to have been caught. So pissed that she didn't realize I myself had been staring at her the entire time in order to catch the moment she turned back.

"Hello!" Flo said when she noticed me staring into Maggie's seatback. "Where have you disappeared off to?"

"Sorry, nowhere," I said. "Just thinking of everything I'll need to do"

Telling Flo that I was going to Iraq brought back all kinds of memories about Maggie, and so when I'd seen her that first night at dinner, after just having told Flo a couple days before, I felt an urgency and importance in that chance meeting that overwhelmed me.

Even before Maggie had landed back into my life, the deployment meant I was going to break things off with Flo. These kinds of major life changes forced me into thinking farther ahead than any normal relationship would require. How could I ask her to wait a year for me, then break things off after that?

I'd seen guys do it, and it was horrible on the partner. I wasn't going to waste a year of Flo's life that way. I had to know if I was in it for the long haul with Flo and the answer was no. I couldn't picture popping the question, walking down the aisle, having kids. Or rather, when I did, it was Maggie's face I saw. Which made me feel like a terrible shit.

As it stood, pre-Maggie shock dinner, I had begun to explain to Flo that I was going to end things.

"I don't want to leave you here, waiting for me if things between us aren't going to go the long haul. And so—"

Flo cut me off. She literally flattened her palm on my lips. "Not yet," she'd said. "One devastating bit of information at a time, okay?"

Incredibly strange, I thought. Didn't everyone prefer the Band-Aid method? And besides, how could you continue on with your everyday life knowing someone was about to drop a bomb on you?

Since I was the bad guy here, I nodded and kept my thoughts to myself.

We were in training and peacekeeping mode for a handover

to the Iraqis, which looked like it was never going to happen. The position meant a promotion. Colonel was a pretty big deal. But I also knew it was one step closer to sacrificing the next decade of my life with the most likely outcome of being asked to leave when I was finally near enough to the top to truly believe I might get there.

Army had given me a lot—the best, most loyal friends a guy could have, a look at the world, an incredible education, a chance to make a difference. It had made me a man. But I thought I might have been given all I would get.

But the promotion meant more money. It was a no-brainer. If I was going to leave, this would be the perfect final job for me. I'd already made the decision to accept the position and break things off with Flo days before I realized that Flo's friend Maggie was *my* Maggie.

If I'd been honest with myself, I'd flirted with the possibility from the first time she'd mentioned her new work colleague months back. But I'd decided it wasn't her. Or more honestly, I'd decided if it was, I wasn't ready to know what to do with that. I'd been slowly readjusting my world view since Maggie, telling myself we had only been that intense because we were young, I was overseas, there was a whirlwind, *take this girl across the globe to be with me* element to it.

I was nearly starting to believe that I could be okay with blander relationship expectations the next time around. There had to be a middle ground between the wasteland that was my relationship with Flo and the fire that had been my incredible life with Maggie.

But after the dinner with Maggie, I'd been selfish. I hadn't been thinking about Flo, even if I'd tried. I'd been wrong to try to rationalize away what I'd had with Maggie. After all these years, here it still was. And it was the real thing.

I tried to bring myself to finish that conversation with Flo, but I hadn't. I knew *trying* was for weak people. I could have. I didn't. And that was awful, even if the reason was that Maggie and anything to do with her blinded me to everything in sight. It had always been that way. Was it a relief when Maggie asked me not to talk to Flo then? Not really, because now things had gone on too long and it needed to be out. But I'd respect Maggie's needs. That was the main reason I'd fucked things up the first time around.

Now, I couldn't deny my body was rejecting the idea of deployment: I didn't want to go, despite the fact I'd already told Flo I was. What I had to work out was whether I listened to every fiber of my being, and despite the fact that she may never have me, stay home for Maggie, or just suck it up, realize I'd lost my chance with her, and go on deployment.

It didn't feel like much of a choice. Even if I was risking everything on the gamble she'd have me back, it was a no-brainer to leave the army, the extra pension money the higher rank would afford (which no one left on the table), detonate Flo's world, and give it a go with Maggie because even if it didn't work out, I needed Maggie to know she was worth more to me than anything else in this world. I wasn't going to make that mistake again. Leaving Maggie to go to Afghanistan all those years ago was my greatest regret.

So what was I doing here with Flo pretending I was filling in yet another round of security clearance papers? Maggie had asked me not to say anything yet, and I had to respect her wishes if I had any hope of making things right. Because as determined and cocky as I was, I knew there was a slim chance of anyone emerging from this love triangle in good shape.

Would Maggie have me? In the end, I truly didn't know. I'd failed her, and that was about the worst thing I could do to her after dragging her across the globe. Why should she ever trust me again, especially when she'd forged such an incredible friendship with Flo, who she *could* count on? Who counted on *her*.

Still, I couldn't help thinking Flo would be mortified if she'd stood in the way of the happiness of two people she cared for so greatly. I would in her shoes. It was a cluster-fuck. And there was a reason people had come up with that term.

All of this was based on a feeling that Maggie could open her heart again to me. Because I thought I could see in her eyes and read in her words her desire that she wanted to, that this wasn't just lust or a bit of fun, or an exciting venture into what-if territory.

In my world, feelings didn't get much of a say—*unless* everything in the fact-based world was no longer reliable. So I couldn't say I was "sure" she would have me, but I was as close to sure as one could get without having a signed statement. I was *bacon* sure. And that was a pretty good indicator, if you'd been there for that ridiculously hot and heavy time. Which I had.

So, when my feeling said, *go to the conference, talk to Maggie,* I had no choice but to listen. It was the only way to get to the facts, wasn't it? And I had to behave honorably as I hunted out the truth. Which meant Maggie was off-limits for now, despite the sensual draw of her lips, her body, her irresistible sexting, on-board staring, everything. There was such a thing as honor. But it didn't stop me from steaming with jealousy every time I thought of her sitting with someone else and anger when he exhibited how unappreciative of Maggie he was.

So that's exactly where my mind was as I found myself in that aisle seat, my leg stretched out because it felt that tiny bit closer to her; my skin was on fire. I wanted her so badly. All through the flight, that fucking Reg's head was visible over the seat back and it felt like a sty in my eye.

I'd put together the packet of all my paperwork I needed to complete for the deployment, and I told Flo I had plenty of work to keep me busy while she was in her sessions and meetings. Hopefully that would get me out of QT with Reg. And it would give me a back-up plan if it ended up that going to Iraq was the right move because Maggie told me to go fuck myself, I'd lost my chance and she'd never have me back.

Even then, I didn't think I would be able to give up on her. And yet, my instinct was to fill out the papers, keep the process ticking over. The momentum to do so came from somewhere deep inside, and I worried this was a place that knew things could never work out with Maggie, so I held back from questioning it too much, and instead chalked it up to a lifetime of preparedness and tried to believe that.

Amazing, then, that I wasn't filling out any of the papers, huh? Instead, I was doing a number on the boarding pass with my fist and obsessing over the brief interaction I'd had with Maggie in the Qantas Airline Lounge before the flight. "Bet you're going for that bacon. A whole plate of it," Maggie said. She'd turned red immediately following the words, as if she'd forgotten for a second that we weren't together anymore. I'm sure those text messages weren't much help. We were at the complimentary buffet and she had a clean plate.

My mouth had quirked at the serotonin jolt. I was euphoric remembering our early days of all-day sex, running out of all the necessities because we couldn't keep our hands off each other. *Bacon.* I shouldn't eat it, I thought, because it was going to feel like an ex-rated show I was putting on for all the waiting travelers. This is what she'd always done to me. But I was a man of extraordinary control. At least, I used to be.

"You got me," I said, my eyes locked onto hers, both of us zigzagging our gazes in synchronicity. Was she sending me a message? She'd been pretty clear she wasn't going in that direction. But her body language and words said something different. Perhaps she was in the same boat as me: couldn't help it.

Thankfully, Maggie didn't tong the greasy strips onto my plate. My physical reaction to that would have meant an emergency run for the toilets until things calmed down in my jeans. I could already feel myself getting restricted in there and took a deep breath to cool things down. Still, when she turned away, I pinched a whole shitload onto my plate. What the fuck was I doing? *Playing with fire.*

Back at the table of two star-crossed couples, I tried to stare at the newspaper, hoping nobody would realize I couldn't be reading without my eyes moving, wouldn't realize I was thinking things like "star-crossed."

"Oooooh, bacon! Can I have a piece?" Flo asked. I wanted to say no. That was my bacon. What was she doing stealing my bacon when that bacon was posing as my sublimated sexual contact with Maggie to keep me from doing anything worse? Why in the world did she have to have *this* bacon out of all the bacon in the world? This was getting incredibly fucked up, and we hadn't even gotten off the ground yet.

"Of course," I managed to say. But I couldn't watch her eat it. My eyes didn't budge from the headline "ScoMo Fumbles Football." There was a hollowness carved into my chest. I couldn't even enjoy a good jab at the Prime Minister. I rode the bittersweetness of the pain, the euphoria, and as I sank my teeth into the salty perfection, I rode the crescendoing waves of it all through the memory, much-referenced as of late, of Maggie and me frying bacon when she'd emigrated. The two of us in our little bungalow we'd been lucky enough to rent at the beach in Coogee. She was in my tee shirt, which was riding up on her pert ass in a way that drove me crazy.

I'd come up behind her while she wielded the tongs and kissed her neck. Now, I felt my stomach drop as I conjured up the temporary insanity I'd experienced at the beginning of our relationship. The break from reality as I quickly picked up the tempo of the movements of my body against hers. I'd had to have her. Had to please her and have her and have her and please her. The two were the same. And the wave was crashing over me again.

As I stared out the window at the cargo crew carelessly tossing luggage onto the plane we were about to board, I caught Maggie's reflection and knew from the way she moistened her lips and swallowed that she was thinking the same thing. Bad as we were behaving, I'm not going to lie, I was ridiculously turned on.

I turned back to the paper. But not before I flashed her one private look that I hoped said everything I was feeling.

"Look at Lionel pretending to read the paper," Maggie said. What was she trying to do? Surely, she knew the effect she had on me.

When I looked up, I breathed in too quickly and a bit of bacon lodged itself in my throat. I began to choke.

"Here, here." Flo held out a glass of water. I hesitated before I took it. Her gesture and my acceptance seemed so loaded with meaning. I was a total cock. And yet, my fire wasn't extinguished. I recognized this juncture of desperately wanting to do both the right and the wrong things. It was a dangerous, incredible place. But it never ended well.

TWELVE

MAGGIE

SHE WAS the absolute worst friend in the world. Why had she said that thing about the bacon? And then made it worse with that comment about George not reading the paper, which would undeniably illustrate that she was thinking all the same things she'd been thinking during the sexts, only now they were thrown together at a beautiful beach resort for two days and nights.

Danger. Danger. She'd put in so much time and planning to ensure she didn't say or do anything that would encourage any lingering feelings or attraction while they were all together here. How had she come out with all that right from the outset? Because she couldn't help herself.

She knew he'd go straight to memories of their old cottage in Coogee. She'd bought him that shirt that said *Bacon.* And that was because it was their thing—not sex and candy, but sex and bacon. It was a naughty thing and it had gotten to the point where one or the other of them only had to think the word, or conjure the smell, and they'd be headed for a bathroom stall, or a car, or once, even a rock formation on the beach.

Euphoria and impulsiveness had made her feel they'd got it

right back then. Right in the way most people only dreamed about. And because he was often away for work, that stage of their relationship lasted longer than for most people.

Four months into her Australian life, she was waiting for the other shoe to drop. But it hadn't. If anything, George's home-comings became more frenzied occasions. Her desperate hunger for him sated in ever-increasing displays of lust-fulfillment. She had to explore every bit of him, plant her flag. But it was never enough. Crazed was the way that phase of their lives was. Deliciously crazed.

She woke one morning to realize she hadn't made any friends in Sydney. She'd barely managed to keep contact with her father or stepmother. For the first time since before boarding school, Maggie had ignored her rules about keeping a bag packed. Why hadn't she seen this?

She was playing with fire allowing herself to get so attached to her life with George. And she needed to protect herself. Because what they had wasn't going to work out. Not something as greedy, powerful, and intense as this. There'd be a huge explosion at the end of their short fuse, and she needed to start damage control. Because the only thing she was certain of was that there'd be plenty of destruction. And then came the deployment announcement.

They weren't conscious, the changes she'd made after that. But George was no typical guy. He picked up on slight deviations. He intuited what they meant. He was the most intelligent person she'd ever met—both intellectually and emotionally, and there was very little she could get away with and remain under his radar.

She'd pushed him away. What a thing to come natural to someone. Maggie was not one to dwell on how fucked up that made her, but . . .

She'd come here intent on fixing things with Reg, and here

she was, her mind completely eclipsed by sex and bacon, her best friend who she shared a career with, her romantic relationship teetering on the edge, and therefore everything hanging in the balance. What had she been thinking with that get-it-out-of-your-system-with-sexts theory? All it had done was increase the feeling of foreplay between them. Her body was reacting like they were already in the middle of having sex.

Maggie couldn't articulate what all these feelings meant, but she had the worst feeling that George could. And this terrified her. She could draw a line in the sand. But she sensed he could wipe that away in an instant. It would be difficult to do the right thing. But it always was. She could and *would* handle difficult.

BACK IN HER room after a welcome lunch chock-a-block with fresh mango and seafood, and a short employee-only meeting focused on the investors, Maggie did her best to do up all the hooks and ties of the lingerie she'd packed for Reg. Somehow, the bacon mishap and the trying not to look at George over her prawns and tropical fruit like he was the second course had doubled her determination to blow and blow until she could rekindle a fire between herself and Reg.

And so she was glad this lingerie was Reg stuff, a slutty cheap netting number in bright colors that presented exposed parts of her body as if they were Michelin-chef baked tartelettes that people waited three years for the pleasure of paying hundreds of dollars for. She took a look in the mirror and tried not to listen to the voice in her head that told her she wasn't crazy; she'd been with Reg three years and people built family empires on less than that. *But not desperate, once-in-a-lifetime love.*

When Maggie emerged from the bathroom, pulling off her best hair flip, he was lying with his back to her, looking asleep.

Worse, she sensed he was pretending. The snore had an artificial perfection to its cadence she didn't recognize.

She felt rejected and like there was an ending she needed to face. All she had to do was look down at her Dayglo ringed nipple to prove that. There was the George factor shining a terrifyingly alluring and destructive light over it all. She made herself take deep breaths so her resentment, disappointment—mainly in herself—and her incredible frustration would subside.

All she wanted was to go down to the bar and get wasted. But that was too dangerous. There was the fancy dinner after this and she would need all of the self-control she could muster. So why did she decide to let Reg sleep instead of waking him to go to the ballroom with her? Even she couldn't buy her logic any longer. Was it any wonder her attempt to get sexy with Reg had turned out this way?

She poured herself one small glass of the white wine they'd bought at the airport duty free and sat outside on the balcony. What would happen if she let things go where her heart kept weaseling its way back to? *Um, sorry, Flo. I'm in love with your boyfriend. And he's in love with me. This all happened years ago, and somehow we've caught you up in all this. Think we can still be friends? Maybe you can be bridesmaid at my wedding?*

Obviously, it was going to be more like Maggie lost a friend, and then put her trust in George again, only to lose him too. But only after she tread the path of "wait until all the decisions were made for you and you'd hurt everyone in the process," rather than being out with it.

LOOKING OUT TO THE ENORMOUS, nearly full moon so low in the sky she had the urge to reach her fingertips out to it, Maggie recalled those early Coogee days, George introducing each of the local specialties—culinary, cultural, architectural, and natural—in his own articulate mix of information and mood, which seemed to stain these details ever after.

And despite trying her best to avoid that pulsing inside drawing her to it, George and his bloody beautiful, low-hanging moon took her back to George and sex, sex and bacon, sex in the bacon tee shirt. Without the tee shirt. Jeez, she was worked up. It was time to get ready and she was so full of hormones she couldn't bring herself to put her lovely dress on and head down and pretend to be a good friend and girlfriend.

The only way to settle her mind was to look at it like this: what was in her head and on her phone couldn't hurt anyone if she'd drawn a hard line under the real-world exchange, promising to never repeat anything like it again. But as she tucked a lipstick, room key, and her phone inside her purse—the first one she'd bought here in Australia for George's friend's wedding in the Hunter Valley—she wasn't so sure of her logic.

Thankfully, the ballroom had been set for one of those hokey mixer kinds of dinners where you had to sit with a different person every course. Then there were a couple of guest speakers, and down the course list, she could see even the post-dinner drinks were mitigated by rules—you had to sit with this one and then that one, trying cocktails inspired by the latest ingredients, taste some blindfolded, all that.

Throughout the first two rounds of awkward, forced dinner conversation, in which her gaze wandered the room trying not to look at George, searching for Flo, Maggie's guts churned. Where *was* she? Had George told her after all? Was she on a plane home, now, writing an awful letter to Maggie about how betrayed she was? The idea opened a Molotov cocktail of emotions and regrets, namely the ignition she'd added to it all with her stupid bacon comment and George's intense reaction. *Dumb.*

Had she no self-control? And if she was so worried about

what she said, why was she still thinking about it, still feeling it, every slight movement of her body feeling erotic and electric as if everyone could see how turned on she was?

She flicked her hair off her shoulder in just such a charged-up way, imagining how that sex bubble might be alleviated with a meeting in one of the dark corners of this hotel when no one was looking, when she located her MIA friend Flo in the flesh.

Flo was inexplicably manning the front table and seemed to be enjoying herself. Maggie knew Flo's flirtation signals and she was giving them out to a man who wasn't George, a move she'd confront her about in any other situation. Which just went to show the foundation of their friendship had already shifted. Another guilt pang to avoid during *What are your five strengths and what are mine and how could we work together as a team?*

Maggie forgot the name of the guy she sat next to, something incredibly Australian like Clancy or Percy. And the nametag would have helped, but he'd "cleverly" turned it back to front.

"See who's really paying attention," he said.

Not me. Maggie tried to navigate the forced social interaction with an array of *yous, your teams,* and worst of all *you who,* which certainly settled the reality for Clancy or Percy. Thankfully within seconds, it was time to move onto someone who hadn't manipulated their nametag.

It wasn't George, but George was sat right across the table, with Clancy/Percy, and she swore she could feel the temperature rise the moment he sat down. Oh, he smoldered. His look said he hadn't wavered one bit and that this bit of ridiculousness he had to take part in to show her that was fine by him. Or at least that's what she imagined.

She caught herself staring as George reached across and turned Clancy's (aha!) nametag the right way. She could make out from her best lipreading the words "Looks like you have this the wrong way 'round."

Maggie smiled. George had always made things seem so simple. Sometimes she wondered if that was the reason he'd gone to Afghanistan so soon after her move Down Under. he simply assumed they were meant to be and so they'd pick up where they left off when he returned. But then she'd switch perspectives. Surely he'd know emotions, especially hers, weren't so easily set into lockstep.

"Earth to Maggie," her latest skills-pairing partner, Kimberly Prott, from marketing said, waving a hand in her face. Instinctively, she turned. George had seen. The smolder sprouted a smirk. *Okay, I give up,* she felt like yelling and storming over to get it on with him.

"Apologies, don't know where I'd gone off to," she said.

"Well, I do. Tall, light, and handsome at twelve o'clock. Shit, Flo has got herself one hot man."

"I guess. If you like that sort of thing."

Kimberly sprayed her mouthful of bubbles over the table in front of her. "Sorry," she said. Thankfully, her own embarrassment derailed further inquiry. "Let's get on with the ridiculous team building. So, do you know how to fix a car?"

Oh God, how had her life come to this?

Maggie excused herself to see why Flo was manning the entrance.

"What are you doing over here?" Maggie asked.

"Cynthia meant to do it, but she got a bad case of gastro and begged me to fill in." Flo shrugged. "At least everyone will get to see how hot I look in this dress."

God, did she. Embroidered sequins in a flapper style suited her long, straight body. Her hair snaked over her right eye in the finger waves she often wore for dressy events. "You look incredible. Why didn't I see you here before?"

Flo shrugged. "Been here." She was lying. But who was Maggie to point that out? She must have had her reasons. She knew not everything was about *her*, but separating out what did and what didn't have to do with her was getting incredibly difficult to do.

"Right back atcha. Why are you here stag?"

"Reg didn't feel well," she lied. He was probably gorging on room service and watching some dumb superhero movie.

"Well, I'm sure you saw Lionel's over there—"

Maggie shrugged. What was that meant to say? *Of course,* she'd seen him. He was at her table. She added a vigorous nod with a knowing eye crinkle. *Much better. Jeez.*

"He's wanting to kill me for bringing him to this event and not talking to him, although that's pretty standard for us these days. Probably having a better time up here than I would sitting at our table anyway—you know this forced-mixing bit is wrapping up. I still need to do some of Cynthia's jobs. Hand stuff out when people leave, blah, blah.

"So why don't you go and sit with Lionel? Maybe he'll stop giving me the stink eye." She was telling untruths again. George hadn't been looking at her; and she hadn't even been here for him to look at. Maggie had been watching. Anxiously. And besides, he wasn't a stink-eye kind of guy. He'd always mocked Maggie when she flashed hers, said she had "facial Tourettes," which was true.

Flo pointed behind her toward the far corner of the room, the round table alongside the plate glass wall where they'd both just been sitting. She still had the smell of him in her nostrils. She might even have been high on it. Like a drug addict.

"Let me know what gets him talking. I could use some pointers," Flo said. "And don't you spend a minute thinking about what Reg is doing. We'll worry about that tomorrow. You look too gorgeous to pine over him. His loss. In fact, if I were you, I'd get up to a little bit of trouble. Maybe Lionel can be your wingman."

Maggie nearly fell over when she delivered that with a wink. She could feel her face heat while she nodded. "Thank God for you, Flo." And she meant it, pointing a proverbial gun at the tears that threatened. *This is your own fault. And you don't seem to be doing anything to stop it.*

"Don't I know it?" Flo smiled. "If only there was a man who could be like you."

Maggie gleamed despite the turmoil. She knew just what her friend meant. Which was a big part of why she was so hesitant to move forward with these gut-wrenching feelings for George. She walked around the table and bent over her friend to give her a squeeze. This sucked.

From behind her hair, she could hear Flo. "Okay, okay, I get it. Stop being so American. I know you love me."

"Right, sorry." Maggie tried not to look at George across the room, but it was difficult. She had a homing instinct for him, and he must have had one for her, because he was staring her down in a way that made her look away, and then, helpless against the impulse, look back to make sure he was still watching.

She hadn't allowed herself to create words from the feelings stirring in her hollow heart since the day George walked out of her life, but they were front and center as she traced the path to him.

I love you. Trying to forget you is pointless. The harder I try, the worse the ache.

Those thoughts were not helping her stay strong through what she was about to walk into—a perfect storm.

This walk from Flo to George was going to be it, wasn't it? How could any of them walk out of here the way they'd walked in? It didn't seem possible. Especially with Flo leaving the two of them alone with her blessing, all that was unspoken between them, Reg's rejection of her final action plan fresh. Maggie knew her resolve had worn down. She knew if George tried anything on (she loved that Aussie term of phrase), she wouldn't be able to resist. And she hated herself for it.

She was two tables away when Ken from the art department stood in her path. "You. Look. Well—I'd better not finish that if I don't want to get in trouble with HR. I was hoping to get paired up with you."

"Thank you. You don't look so bad yourself." Ken was slim, decent height, excellent movie-star hair. She was going to let the flirting slide.

"Don't tell me you're here alone?"

"No, she's with me." George was behind her, his hand tender on her arm. She couldn't speak. She couldn't move. Why had he touched her that way? It gave his words a whole new connotation. Was he not worried what got back to Flo?

She reminded herself Ken didn't know her or Flo well enough to understand there was anything out of the ordinary at play.

"My bad," Ken said.

"As long as it doesn't happen again," George said, and led her the rest of the way to the table. A foot away, she realized what she should have done and tugged her arm, hard, from his grip.

"Really? You expect me to buy that?" he said. She was glad he couldn't see her expression. "There's no use fighting it, Mags."

At the table, he moved a place card and plucked Maggie's from her former seat to stand in its stead. Then he pulled out the corresponding chair alongside his. Kimberly's jaw was on the floor.

Maggie gave George what she hoped, and feared, wasn't anything near to a death stare.

"Still haven't perfected that, I see."

That cracked her. She couldn't help a corner of her mouth rising. That used to be a thing with them. She'd try to show she didn't need him, didn't love him nearly as much as he thought she did. And she'd fail miserably. He was better at it. It used to scare her. Very much. And she hadn't liked that.

And when he left, she told herself she'd been right not to like it. It hadn't been his military training or a way to cover a show of weakness the way she sometimes convinced herself. It had been just what it appeared on the surface: George didn't love her nearly as much as she thought he did.

What was probably happening here was a case of wanting what he couldn't have. And when he could? What then? She'd be right back where she'd been, terrified of his not needing her, pushing him away, until it worked, and he was gone.

She swallowed. What in the world was she doing here trying to sort through all that? Setting herself up for a second round?

"Champagne?" he asked, lifting the bottle from the ice bucket.

"Yes, please."

"Where's Rog?"

"Reg."

"Whatever. He's an idiot if he let you out of the room alone looking like that."

She didn't want to like his words so much and relied a bit on her champagne to cover the feelings. Nearly drained the glass in one sip.

"So, what's new with you?" she asked the way a new friend might.

He smirked. God, she hated it when he was onto her.

"Lionel!" Out of nowhere was Flo. "I hope you're telling Maggie what a dickhead Reg is."

"As a matter of fact, I was."

Maggie shot him a look. Again with the smirk.

Flo said, "I have to get back in a minute, but I wanted to check on you." She hugged Maggie from behind. There was no denying the exchange of mutual emotion. Maybe now that George had seen that, he'd get it and stop with the smirking, put a stop to the whole thing, because Lord knew she didn't have the willpower to do it.

"Love you," she said in Maggie's ear, then kissed George on the cheek. Maggie knew what kissing George felt like, and that was all wrong. A chill went down her back. She felt terrible for both of them. There was nothing worse than knowing someone wouldn't miss you when you left . . . except being the person to inflict that on someone to whom you wanted to do anything but hurt, especially when that person was dreaming of your best friend.

As she turned to watch Flo's shimmery silhouette shrink to the entrance table, Maggie surprised herself by verbalizing her thoughts.

"We are both going to hell."

"We're not going to hell. Love is ugly and messy. It doesn't respect boundaries."

"Right." He said the L word again and she panicked. "And besides, we both know you only want me because you can't have me," Maggie said.

It was his turn to jolt back. Clearly she'd had it wrong. But that didn't change anything, did it? Oh, please say it didn't change anything. If she gave in, it would only end in disaster, and the return of her gut wrenching. She didn't want to go back there.

Unable to eat, unable to concentrate, unable to decide what to do next. It was unbelievable Reg had been attracted to her when she'd been so . . . so *nothing*. She had nothing to contribute to the relationship. But recently, she had. And most likely, that's where her dissatisfaction with Reg had truly gained the kind of momentum she needed to go.

She'd bet good money he'd find someone else so desperately damaged that he could be everything to them—without even trying—the way he'd been for Maggie. Maybe he had already. They were so distant, she wouldn't be shocked.

"Maggie. *Maggie*."

No, don't look at me and say my name like that. She reached for the champagne and topped off her glass only. It was rude, but she felt at this juncture even something as innocent as filling his glass would encourage him in the wrong direction. Even worse, she suspected he knew she was thinking that.

"Maggie, what?" She was acting like a bratty teenager.

George quirked a brow. "We both know I *can* have you. And I will. But we can play it your way if you want." He spoke close, quietly, words for only the two of them.

"And what way is that?" she asked.

"Oh, you know. Pretend we're going to reject our feelings because it's too messy and too inconvenient, and instead, continue on this wrong-footed path we've both been on since our split."

"We're not doing that." They were so doing that.

"*Oh*-kay."

"But the thing is we *have to*." She stared at Flo across the hall to underline the reason.

"If you know Flo as well as I think you do, I'm sure you know she wouldn't appreciate that kind of condescension, that baby hand-holding. She cares for you. I know she does. She'd want you to be happy."

It certainly wouldn't be tied up in a neat package, but ultimately he was right. "But she also wouldn't appreciate her best friend and her boyfriend getting together behind her back."

His look said he knew she was right, too.

They sat in silence for a long moment.

"Have one dance with me. And then we won't talk about this anymore tonight."

He stood, pulled Maggie up by her hand. His smell, his eyes so intensely focused on her, his fingers strong and reassuring on hers. She longed to press her lips to his, to give into the desire running molten through her. For a second she stood there, letting the sensation wash over her, then she turned reflexively to Flo, who stood and waved Maggie toward the dancefloor, no doubt believing the *wingmanning* was about to start. With a heavy heart as fluttery and hollowed out with aching as it had been in a long while, she let George lead her to the dance floor. Oh, how the memories flooded back.

There was a good crowd out there. The band was playing Australian classics that George had oriented her to. All the songs on her *George* Spotify playlist. Was the whole world in on this?

The song was *Whenever I Fall*, by Crowded House. Even when George was no longer a part of her life, she swooned when she heard it, worked herself into such emotion, the only thing that would chase it away was furious exercise. The fastest bike ride she could muster. And even then, she was playing it on repeat, high on all the memories bombarding her now.

Here under the low lights with George, his hand in the more friendly dance position—thank God for that—he looked at her in that penetrating way he had, broadcasting clear as day that his feelings mirrored hers. God, he was gorgeous, even more so when the smolder was this close up.

His ice-blue eyes appeared to reach all the way to his soul. It was no wonder she was lost in them. The whiskered lines that had formed around them since he'd been her George only enhanced the effect. Fuck, she was toast. For a moment, she closed her eyes and gave into the tsunami of pure feeling.

Their sway was effortless. This was so much better than talking, and so much worse because these were not words that could be explained away. Responses such as these were real, undeniable—she'd faked enough of them with Reg to know the difference. Now she looked back at herself in those situations with shame. Hadn't she realized she was doing Reg—and herself —a terrible disservice?

"Come close," he said.

She shook her head.

He slid his lower hand, alongside her waist, to her back. It didn't take much to pull her toward him. She closed her eyes. She couldn't have him seeing right through her this near. He'd know everything, and then there'd be no chance for her.

"You're my favourite."

Her eyes flashed open.

"That's what it is," he continued on. "I used to struggle to work out exactly what it was about you that makes me love you so. But you're my favorite everything. There is literally nothing I want besides you."

Not *made* me love you. *Makes* me love you.

"I should go."

"If you leave now, it would look suspicious."

"No. What we're doing now is suspicious. A blind man could see what's happening here."

"Please, don't go." His hand tightened on the small of her back.

"George, I have to. Don't contact me while we're here. It's too intense. I have a busy day here tomorrow. But if we do see each other, it's as Flo's friend and partner. Nothing more."

"No. You can't keep doing this. What's between us is undeniable. You keep trying to fight it when we're apart, but you can't. What you're going to wind up doing is hurting Flo more, not to mention you." He squeezed tighter. "And me." If his gaze was penetrating before, it was jackhammering his intentions now. "You have to tell her. Or you have to let me tell her. Which is it going to be?"

He was so right. That was exactly what she was doing. And pretty soon it was going to get worse. The sexting was going to give way to the real thing and where would they all be then?

"No. You're wrong. This is it. Not just for this trip. But once and for all. There's a reason I can't bring myself to tell her." *More than one actually.* "And so, I think we should call this what it is—things coming to a natural end. Again." *Oh, I so didn't mean that.* And yet, there it was, coming out of her mouth. Perhaps her heart hadn't caught up to her brain's logical conclusion yet. And for a second, after getting the words out, she felt lighter than she had since the night he'd come back into her life. Surely that must mean she was doing the right thing.

He held onto Maggie's hand as if that touch could say everything, undo the words she'd just said, and he'd be right to place money on that, because the jolt of sensation went straight to her chest where regret at her words and desire for him swept away the relief in an instant. *I didn't mean it,* she longed to say. But she had to trust her instinct.

Maggie began to pull away. At first he held tight, wouldn't let her go, his gaze echoing the sentiment. But eventually, he could see she was determined, and he allowed her hand to slip from his grasp. Letting him go was the wrong thing. That was clear as day. So why was she still going? Because not only was it morally wrong, this entangled situation, it was also terrifying to be presented with a do-over of something that had caused her so much pleasure and then so much pain. This was always going to hurt. She was kidding herself if she thought anything else.

It took every ounce of control not to look back. *You're*

protecting yourself. She made it to the entrance, and the tears she shed in front of Flo were real, so it wasn't hard to convince her this evening was just too difficult for her, that she needed to go to bed.

And then there was the air outside, a tropical flower scent. Then the warmth of the night and the stars George had walked her through all those years ago, slightly different from this perspective, which made her wonder about symbols.

She breathed in the eucalyptus of the damned stringy bark trees, now layered over the frangipani, trees which he'd made sound so incredibly beautiful that she never walked past one without thinking about him.

She stayed out there long enough that she knew Reg would be well and truly asleep before she slid into bed. She looked up at their room's window to check the television was no longer playing shadows on the walls just to be sure.

THIRTEEN

GEORGE

I HAD to talk to Maggie. Last night had gone all wrong.

Ever since the dinner, I had been after the perfect opportunity to put Maggie at ease, to get us onto the right track. And what did I do when I actually had the opportunity? I went too fast and scared the hell out of her. At breakfast the next day, I was going to find out where she was headed and meet her outside whichever conference room she'd eventually emerge from, but Maggie had breakfast in her room.

I hoped it wasn't to avoid me, though I was pretty sure it was. Although I couldn't ignore the possibility it had something to do with that jackass, Reg. Especially since he came down without her. Just the sight of him got my hackles up.

I took my plate of bacon to his table where Flo had placed her handbag and laptop, where his face was buried in his phone. "Rog," I said and sat down, waving at Flo, who I explained to the top of his head, was waiting for one of those olive bagels she was fainting over to complete its toaster cycle.

He rolled his eyes.

I hated him.

"Reg," he said.

I didn't take the bait. "Maggie have a big night?" I asked. Like he would know, douchebag.

"She was out pretty late."

Yeah, with me, dickhead, where she belongs. I nodded. Surely he realized we'd noticed Maggie had been forced to go solo because he was being a wanker for whatever wanker reason he had. Still, he didn't feel the need to address that. "She okay?"

"Yup. She's a workaholic. Had to fix something. Out of some kale or something. You know, a proper emergency."

Dick. "Mmm-hmmm."

Bagel toasted and spread with cream cheese, Flo sat across from me next to Reg. She'd heaped some steamed greens alongside the bagel, and I recognized the child-like curiosity in her expression. This was my favorite thing about Flo—she always dug into whatever she came into contact with, like the world was a place of mystery and she took it on as her personal mission to solve it.

Sometimes she asked too many questions. But this occasion wasn't one of them. The three of us sat in silence for a moment while the dining room hummed around us. Outside the entrance in the beach front space, the sky was clear, sun shining, and kids wielded swimming rings and goggles. I felt miles from Flo and in disbelief that I'd allowed things to get here.

She'd once asked me if she was a rebound relationship, and I'd said no. That had been a lie. It had been my out. But where to? There wasn't a woman who interested me except Maggie. Flo was wonderful—kind and thoughtful, beautiful and understanding. Why couldn't that be enough?

Whenever I came home thinking I'd get a talking to, she was calm and level-headed. Mostly I didn't deserve it. I owed her better than lying to her. If only I'd understood that then. I understood it now, but promised Maggie I wouldn't say anything. And after last night, I certainly wasn't going to put any more pressure on her.

"Where's Maggie?" she asked.

"Kale emergency, apparently," I offered.

"There was no kale on today's menu," she said. "I'll just text her." An example of the curiosity. Flo buried herself in her own phone, tapping keys, then sighed. No sooner had she lowered the phone to the table than a response dinged.

Flo caught my concerned look. Bless her, she didn't say a word. What did I think she would say? *Curious about what I'm typing because you're in love with my best friend?* But she did raise the screen close to her face so I couldn't see, which made me suspicious. Had Maggie finally gone and done it? Not over text message, surely.

Whatever she read made Flo laugh out loud. I never made her laugh like that anymore. She lay the phone on the table, face down, and shook out her wide hairdo. It didn't take an idiot to see how deep their friendship ran. There was real happiness in that laugh. God, I hated myself for the thoughts I couldn't stem. If I was a smarter man, I'd say it was time to throw in the towel, move onto a sub-Maggie relationship with someone new, and prepare myself for an average, unsatisfying life.

"Apparently, it *was* kale related," she dead-panned, looking at me in an unreadable way. Another alternative presented itself. Had she worked out that Maggie was my ex on her own? Maybe *I* was a bigger dick than *Reg*. If there was no Maggie friendship involved, I would be out with it right now, over the steamed greens and the olive bagel. If Reg got hurt in the process, all the better.

Reggie sprung an *I told you so* grin I wanted to smash off his face. No. He was definitely the bigger dick.

"Maggie's going to meet me at the first session. She said maybe you guys could have some guy time at the pool."

Did she now? And if she did, what was she up to? Something that made Flo laugh. Probably in some coded way only the two of them would understand. That was more than a reflection of their connection—a testament to the fact they talked about the both of us. Maggie would know how deeply I'd wanted to steer clear of QT with Reg. What was she up to? "Sorry, Rog. I've got a *lot* of paperwork to sort through. Just here as arm candy."

Flo smiled. "He's off to Iraq next month." It killed me that I'd left it at that, put her through whatever trauma the idea involved without severing ties. I had to end this. Flo was kind and genuine, and had supported me in all the ways that mattered, and what had I done in return? I couldn't say anything to Flo with the way Maggie and I had left things last night, but I could convince Mags to change her stance. I knew I could. And I would.

"Wow. What's that like?" Reg asked.

What kind of answer was he expecting? It was the kind of question someone who didn't have a clue asked. "Things are under better control over there now. We're in handover mode."

That seemed to satisfy him. Probably sent him into scenes from *American Sniper* and *The Hurt Locker*, feeling he *got me.* I wasn't about to talk about drop toilets and fatty American canteen offerings. Reg dove into his omelet. Then he looked up. "Must be hard for Flo, you being overseas like that. In harm's way."

"It's not easy for Flo," I said, feeling the most honest I'd been in a long time.

She looked at me in a way too knowing to mean anything good and then turned to her coffee.

There was silence for a moment, and then Reg started to ask Flo about her bagel. They spent the rest of the hour chattering like a house on fire.

FOURTEEN

MAGGIE

FLO: Guys hating each other. Some kind of testosterone sniffing thing. Guess our future of Easter holidays in Tathra together are not going to happen.

MAGGIE: Me and you can go. Who needs those two? After last night, I'm ready to call it quits with Reg. I think I'm going to do it tonight.

FLO: Really? Oh, he's going to be crushed. Poor thing. I know he's a bit of a wanker, but you could do worse. . .

MAGGIE: Oh no. Has he worked his charms on you? Don't be fooled. They don't last! Three weeks in and it's all video games, Justice League, and forgetting to spray after he's been in the toilet for forty minutes.

FLO: Isn't that just what all guys do?

MAGGIE: You're probably right. It's just that I'm not in love with him, so all of that stuff isn't worth putting up with. Which is why I need to break things off.

FLO: Poor thing. He'll have a hard time replacing you. xo

. . .

MAGGIE MADE a breakfast of instant coffee and tea she'd left to steep too long. She couldn't face either Flo or George after the night she'd had. Why was she sabotaging this second chance with George when he was literally all she wanted in the world? What had Flo made of the distress on her face? Would George give up on this? How many strikes had this been?

When Maggie had woken from the forty minutes of sleep she managed, and had no answers, she knew she had to confront Reg. Things weren't right between them and she needed to cut the ties. She had to trust this path would lead her onto the right one. It was the only choice she had.

She told herself that was the takeaway from last night: one thing at a time. The first step was to break things off with Reg. If she wanted a more fully realized existence, like the kind she'd had with George, she had to put a stop to this lazy survival method she'd bootstrapped together, and getting rid of Reg was priority *uno*. Seeing that dayglo stretchy thing shriveled up on the bathroom floor last night only underlined that.

And she sensed Flo was in the same position. George had been everything to Maggie. But with Flo, she could see that neither of them were better with the other. Instead of co-existing, they seemed to be living side by side, like toddlers did with parallel play. Pull one out and insert someone different and no one would be bothered.

But she was kidding herself if she thought things could reconfigure so easily. To begin with, how could she say anything honest about Flo's situation without fearing that deep down it was probably self-interest driving her to such a point of view?

Being so close to George last night hadn't helped matters. But she had the red line. Now all she had to do was muster the self-control to stick with that. Because that was the right thing to do. The same opposing sentiment that had presented itself last night bloomed in her mind—it didn't *feel* right saying those things to George last night—and wouldn't let her grasp any concrete resolution to her commitment. *One step at a time.*

Still, somehow, she'd made it through the talk on "Incorporating Spelt Flour into Traditional Baking Techniques." She'd even managed to forget the ambient stress and focus for most of the lecture without picturing George at the pool without a shirt on. And though she planned to persevere on the second session, it turned out to be rescheduled. So she found herself with three hours free.

Maggie planned to sit in the sun with a book about Gallipoli. The pool was an intimate rectangle with lovely shady spots care of palms and bright blue umbrellas. Surely, a book about the bloodiest battle in history, read in such luxurious surrounds would put her own problems into perspective, since nothing else seemed to be doing the trick.

Thankfully George was not sunbathing. She would have failed miserably at keeping away from him after she'd been not thinking about him bare-chested for the last forty-five minutes.

She took a free lounge under cover of a pristine umbrella, and within seconds, a pool boy was over with a pair of towels, smoothing one out and keeping one rolled in a perfect cylinder for use as a pillow. Now this was more like it.

She lay back with her knees up and cracked the spine. The book had been a gift from her father when she'd received her Australian citizenship. She hadn't told him George was out of the picture. Mainly because she was ashamed that she'd gone so far from family and everything she knew for a man it hadn't worked out with. He'd inscribed it:

George recommended this book to me the first night you brought him over for dinner. Even if you've read his copy, it seems to me that now you're officially an Aussie, you should have your own. And probably a kangaroo. But couldn't work out how to mail you one of those.

Love,
Dad

SHE'D BEEN SURPRISED to find it in the front pocket of her roller bag this morning because she hadn't used the bag in so many years. Every time she thought to travel home, she found herself unable to click the *Buy* button on the airfare. Oh, she'd hovered the little white arrow, but ultimately chickened out. Google ads retargeting had a field day with her.

But despite her travel hiatus, she'd always had the book tucked in there from before, when she and George were exploring "every state in your new home country" in case whatever she'd brought to read was boring, or she needed a dose of reality and strength.

Today, when she turned the pages, she purposely skipped past the personalized page. It had brought tears to her eyes before. The intro was dense, as she recalled, so she skimmed past that, too, into the first chapter which had a much less academic tone and, eventually, found herself giving into the welcome distraction of reliving the ANZACs most fatal battle of the first World War.

"Maggie?" Kimberly Prott, from marketing, stood over her lounge chair. "Skiving off your lecture?" She wore a smile, but she was the kind of person who probably would rat out Maggie just because. And after her teasing about George the other night, she left a bad taste in Maggie's craw. Her enormous hat looked like it belonged to someone much more fun loving.

"Session was rescheduled, so I have a few hours to spare."

"Mind if I sit next to you? I don't have anything until four."

Wonderful. "Go right ahead. I'm going in for a dip now anyway." Maggie smacked the book shut with a fake smile, as if it didn't kill her to be blocked from her much-needed alone time. There was no way she was getting sucked into one of Kimberly's gossip sessions, especially after her comments last night.

Maggie shed her indigo cover-up and dove in the deep end for laps before she could think about it. By the third arm rotation, she felt her breaths come sharper and more labored. She threw herself into the challenge. Two laps in, Maggie wondered why she didn't do this more often. It was so richly intense.

Her body felt like a cohesive unit, working toward a common goal. How often did it work like that? *Ten laps down.* She could do this all day. Bring on the exhaustion, the full-body deflation. She should have dived in here last night. She felt like she could do anything. *Eleven.*

Her brain conjured an image of George at the end of the pool, holding out a water bottle to her. She felt her focus fracture, her energy suffer. That was why she didn't do this more. Because this was what *they* had done. Together.

Coogee Beach had hosted so many early morning swims for the two of them. She'd felt invincible back then. In a new country, so in love, so deeply satisfied and just living without protecting herself or overthinking anything. Every day a new discovery. Every day George proving to her she'd made the right choice giving herself over to the pull of him.

Look at me all the way on the other side of the world, she'd find herself thinking at odd moments—ordering a flat white or knowing her Australian dress size. God, she was so stupidly happy!

Now she stopped swimming and resorted to paddling to keep herself afloat. With the abrupt halt, her chest heaved painfully.

"Mags." It *was* him, squatting at the edge of the pool, holding out the water to quench her thirst. Accepting it felt X-rated. And like she'd already lost that resolve she'd had last night.

She shook her head.

"Really? You look like you're struggling. I heard you had a late night after you left the party and a kale disaster so, rightfully so."

She grimaced. The dumb excuse she'd given Reg wouldn't have gotten very far with George. He could always tell when she was bullshitting. He said she had a clear tell—she smiled more than usual. Another one of his comments that was always in her head, yanking the ends of her mouth down so she'd be more likely now to be accused of frowning.

Rather than show how spent she was, Maggie pulled herself out of the pool as gracefully as she could. Her white bikini bottom had ridden up, but she wasn't about to pull it back into place. She remembered the effect that gesture had on him. Of course, leaving it with half her ass sticking out wouldn't be very helpful either.

She tried not to run to her chair where a towel was draped over the top. Was she doomed? How was it possible he still had this effect on her after all these years?

She could fight it, though. That was all she could do.

It might help if he could pretend not to watch her toweling off. If he was the one who had begun the charade that they didn't know each other, then he should damn well try to keep it up. Instead he was staring at her like she was a striptease, after saying all those things about being in love with her.

She reminded herself he was a man of integrity. But from here, it felt like she was carrying the entire burden of their secret. And she didn't know if it was merely simpler for him because he didn't have those feelings for Flo any longer, or if he just bore the load better. She was getting fed up with how well he seemed to be handling everything. She remembered her interpretation of that steely exterior of his from their breakup, and she could feel herself beginning to panic. *You don't know what he's thinking,* she reminded herself.

Kimberly watched George approach her lounge chair intently. "Jesus, he is gorgeous. Flo is one lucky girl," she whispered into Maggie's ear as she readjusted the backrest of her chaise and lowered onto it.

"If you're into that sort of thing, I guess," Maggie said louder than she would have liked. She remembered this childish reaction to his steely exterior too. If this was what they did to each other, then maybe the breakup had been for the best.

George's eyebrow quirked and she tugged down the corners of her mouth, just to be sure. Why did she care so much what he thought? *Because you love him too.*

"Mind if I sit here?" he asked, pointing to the lounge on her other side.

He was in a white tee shirt that had an Artillery logo—the old-fashioned wheeled cannon with a crown atop it—on the left front. By his heart. Oh, his heart. She wanted so badly to reach out and touch him there. How could they be standing here so close and yet so ridiculously far away?

She shrugged.

He reached down and pulled his shirt over his head while she and Kimberly watched. *My God, what a body.* She was smacked with the covetousness she used to feel. *This is mine.* What a juvenile way of thinking. So why was she reflexively thinking it now? *Line. Red, red line.* She dragged her gaze from him as he lay beside her. She caught Kimberly's eyes bulge as she fanned her face with her hand.

Maggie did not take Kimberly's bait. She didn't want to pay attention to George, but how could she busy herself so he didn't chat her up? She'd left her phone in the room and she couldn't very well pick up that book, could she, without opening a can of worms. She tucked it farther beneath her chair.

"Watcha reading?" he asked, reaching under to grab it. Where was the personal space? Why had they fallen directly into the joint state they used to inhabit? Hadn't her words last night meant anything? And why wasn't she saying anything to stop him?

George's normally intense gaze went to laser strength as his eye caught the inscription. He knew what it said. When his lids closed, however briefly, she feared for the control they needed here. She knew that heavy blink of his. It was the closest he came to a mental break. Maybe he wasn't so steely after all. She found that this possibility made her more uneasy than his default M.O. If they were both off script, then anything might happen.

He snapped the book shut and squeezed it in his palm, then sat up, pivoted toward her.

"We need to talk," he said.

She could feel Kimberly's sensors beeping wildly behind her.

"Not here," she said.

And that was how they wound up walking along the beach together. It was as if they'd agreed not to speak until they sat upon a rocky outcrop about fifteen minutes later. All the while, they made their barefoot journey along the shore she tried desperately to fight the *déjà vu*.

If he was struggling the way she was, if he was being pulled toward her the way she felt herself pulled toward him, they were in serious trouble.

FIFTEEN

GEORGE

AS I MADE my way along the shore to the rock formation, I told myself I'd have to tell Maggie I was struggling seeing her like this, telling herself this was a natural end. That was bullshit. She knew clear as day we'd made a mistake splitting up, that this cluster-fuck with Flo only underlined that, and that despite what she said, we needed to keep things above-board now, face the music, and then give our life together a real start.

I'd had all night to come up with the right way to say that and yet this moment walking along the beach next to her seemed to say all of that and more, better than words ever could. Neither of us spoke along the walk. It felt like we were afraid to puncture the perfection of the moment with reality. Because from the outside, it looked incredible—clean waves breaking on the shore, kids darting here and there, seagulls hovering for dropped chips and biscuits, the odd regal pelican.

We walked close, following the curved line of washed up shells. They were all that long twisted kind which Maggie used to call *unicorn horns*. I tried not to look there or where our bodies were getting closer, but I could feel when our hands were dangerously close. We used to walk with bits always touching. It wasn't by design. It was instinct. I'd always felt I'd found my other half, the one who made the world make sense. Once we'd found each other, it was impossible to resist. This hadn't changed.

That was why it had been so easy to see the change in her after I told her about the deployment. One day our connection was there, the next, she'd lost that loving feeling, or at least acted as if she did. But that was how it happened, right? I never pretended to put our breakup into a neat box. When people asked why we broke up, I never knew what to say. Usually, I came up with a meaningless, *you know*. That way people could fill in whatever issues they'd already suffered through. It seemed to work. But he wasn't going to let her build that wall between them again. And that meant he had to be careful.

"I'm sure Flo told you things haven't been going so great with us for a while now."

"No." Maggie gave her best Kevlar expression.

"Liar."

Why had he led with that reasoning? That was the most contentious of the ideas he'd come up with, but he kept coming back to the idea that this meant something, that it would convince Maggie that the breakup between him and Flo wouldn't be her fault, and that they could move onto more pressing issues.

She nearly cracked a smile.

"We're going to break up, Mags. Whether or not you're in the picture."

She blew out a huge sigh.

He let that idea sink in. Don't rush, he kept telling himself. There were so many things that needed saying.

"Heard you're a citizen now. Congratulations. So you're sticking around?" I said.

"Yes, I am a citizen. The ceremony was beautiful if—"

She looked at me with those green eyes, and I knew I was the one who'd put the pain in them.

"What? Say it. Please."

"Sad. It was a sad day." She stiffened. I knew how she was about showing weakness.

"I should've been there."

Her head snapped back. She hadn't expected that. "George. Stop."

"Why? Why should I stop if you feel the same? You do. I know you do." *Slow down.* I always got like this around her. Like I had to button everything up because if I didn't, I'd lose my chance. *But there are lots of ways to lose your chance here.*

"But Flo."

"And if Flo wasn't in the picture?"

"She *is* in the picture. And even if there comes a point where she's not in your picture, she's my closest friend. I couldn't ever be with you for that and so many other reasons— my solo citizenship ceremony being only one."

Maggie stopped walking, covered her face in her hands. "I told myself I would not say any of this." It was nearly impossible not to grab for her hand. We both weren't in control of ourselves when we were together. But we were after a common goal. Why was it so hard to get there? My fingers twitched like a command to touch her. In that, we could always make things work.

"I want you to say those things. I *need* you to say those things," I said.

I should have said those things back when. I'd had a long time to realize that. The game we played with being self-contained had an expiration date, and ours had come around. I wanted her to know I understood that. She looked at me, slightly more pained, if possible, but also greatly more desirous, then shook her head, looking incredibly, beautifully sad. God, I needed to touch her.

"George," she said. I couldn't help it; I wiped the tear as it fell from her eye. She held onto my finger with her hand as her eyes closed. I took the chance to graze the skin below her eye with my fingers. Suddenly, she seemed to realize what was happening and she dropped my hand, fell back into her previous cadence, but farther away.

There was a massive rock formation we'd been walking toward, that slate kind, wet with glimmering mineral veins and small cutout pools where tiny crustaceans made their homes. I remembered Maggie lingering for hours around these during her first trips to the New South Wales Coast.

She said everything felt more abundant here in Oz—more colorful, more brilliant, just more. Sometimes I could credit our love with casting that lens because I felt the same way. But it was so gorgeous the way she fell in love with life here that I never argued. After all, she made me see things that way too. How had we let it go so easily?

As we approached the first precarious step toward the plateau, I closed the space between us and reached for her hand without thinking. "Maggie." My muscle memory kicked in. To my relief, she closed her fingers around mine. They seemed to burn right through me. The feel of her small hand wrapped around mine careened me back.

Not unkindly, she slowly pulled her fingers away just as I was riding the high of her touch. This was going to be harder than I thought.

"We can't," she said. "But it was amazing messaging you that way. It felt like the old days, only more. And when you had your hands on me last night—" Oh, did I know what she meant. Maggie picked up her pace, like she had to beat me to the top. I was hopeless in trying not to attach innuendo to that. I was always so turned on when she got to the sweet spot first. I had to stop myself from saying that now.

She sat on the flat portion at the peak of the rock. With the thought of her coming in my head, I sat next to her, then shimmied a few centimetres away, just to be safe. And partially because I wanted her to show me she wanted me as much as I wanted her, thought she might move toward me.

I looked right at her sparkling emerald eyes, which she was desperately forcing toward the shore. As if relenting, she closed her lids for a moment, then trained her gaze on me, shifted toward me. I felt a twitch in my pants. That's all it took. I turned slightly more toward her. *Slowly*, I reminded myself. I had to get her to change her stance on things.

I caressed her cheek with my palm. She responded by nuzzling her skin against my hand. It was the most natural thing in the world.

"Look at us," I said. "This is right."

"Mmmmm," she allowed herself to linger in the sensations, then sighed, straightening, using her own hand to remove mine from her face. "What would be right is if you and I had never split up."

"Right. We'd have a couple kids now, Clancy and Zoe, and I'd be out of the army so I could spend time with all of you, because that's all I want to do."

I leaned in, kissed her on same place my palm had been. Then I trailed my kissed to her ear, where I sucked on her lobe. She moaned the way I'd hungered to hear all this time. And yet, she kept trying to push her "we can't" agenda.

"Are you crazy?" she whispered, breathy. "You can't pop up out of nowhere, drag me into this ridiculous ruse, and then say the kinds of things I've been wanting to hear for the past four years. What about Flo? Do you know what an incredible friend she's been to me? She would never have let me go to my citizenship ceremony alone. And besides, it's too late for all that. I'm well past it. Have been for some time."

My lips feathered along her jawline toward her mouth. She was getting impatient, rotating her face, meeting me halfway.

"You're over me?" I pulled back, teasing her that little bit more.

She shrugged, held out her palms. It was adorable how she tried not to smile. I'd called her on that tell plenty. But it wasn't too late. And this was how I could show her.

Obviously, she was lying about being over me. Exhibit A: the way she moaned and opened her mouth wide for my tongue. That first night at the restaurant on the harbour, in the toilets, there was a sizzle between us. It had grown into a full-on flame. I bent in closer, so she could see what she was doing to me, so I could feel her breasts against my chest. Her mouth took me in all the way, she pressed her hands on the back of my head, as if to say *deeper*. I got it. I needed this connection with her. I don't know how long we were like that. Time had stopped. God, I remember this feeling. I was delirious in it.

"We'll see," I said. Because I'm me. "So here's the thing, Maggie. I am going to tell Flo as soon as we get back." What happened to slowing down? That mouth, those lips, those breasts. That's what happened.

She flinched like I'd hit her. "Just like that?"

"Just like that. I don't think *you* can do it. You want to, but you can't. Which I understand."

"It's not that I can't do it, it's that the reason I'm doing it doesn't feel right."

"It doesn't matter how it feels. That's just you feeling guilty. But we've been through this. Guilty or not, Flo is going to be hurt. But she wouldn't want us to stay apart for her. We aren't in high school. You can't throw away your happiness because it would hurt your friend's feelings. You belong with me. There is nothing more important than that."

I took a gamble here, leaned in close. "I know how vital it is that we're above-board with Flo. We've been through all this. We're going to do this the right way, the best way we can." I tucked a stray strand of hair behind her ear. Oh, that ear! "Right? You with me?"

She didn't speak but she didn't stop me from caressing her silky hair, running my fingers through to the ends, either. Instead, she'd let some of that façade down, she was looking deep into my eyes the way she used to. This was where we put it all on the table, where we were our truest selves, I found myself thinking.

I knew *this*—being with Maggie was the real thing. And I had known those years ago that I shouldn't have gone to Afghanistan. She must have felt so hurt, like she'd wake up one day and I'd just be gone like everyone else in her life. I'd stoked the embers of abandonment she guarded so militantly. She left, and I deployed. Even dropping bombs on bad guys didn't make me feel any better. Anything I said about that now was too little, too late.

Here we were, though, fatefully given a second chance. I couldn't let it go. I wanted to say all those words, but the as soon as I thought them, they seemed to evaporate.

But my issues were only one part of the equation. I wasn't the only person involved here. My words didn't seem to cooperate with the plan. "Well, that's good that you're over me," I said, into her lips, our noses touching. I didn't break eye contact, so we both understood the subtext: we were both full of it. We'd never been in deeper. I pulled away, caressing her hair with my hand.

"And because we're so clearly over each other, it will be easy to stick with my plan. We can't even think about taking anything further with each other until we've untangled ourselves from this situation. And even then, nothing happens until we talk to Flo. Everything legit. I'm going to do everything right this time. And then we can think about getting you back under me where you belong." My cock twitched just from the thought. Before I knew it, I was kissing her again, this time sucking on her velvety bottom lip, drinking in her moans. I told myself this was our last kiss until I was split from Flo.

She said, "We will not be talking to Flo about *us*, because there is no *us* anymore. You will tell her the truth about what we were to each other because this secret is going to destroy our friendship no matter what happens. But she deserves to know the truth—that I haven't just abandoned her because of something she did, or because I don't feel the same way about her."

The subtext stung. I had screwed things up all those years ago because I'd left her and so many things had been left unsaid. But she was dead-on. How could I feel so turned on and so deeply terrible all at once? Why wasn't I saying the right words? I dug deep. "I'm sorry for what happened those years ago," I said in a clumsy, inarticulate attempt. I grabbed her hand. Fuck it. I didn't know a better way to show her how sorry I was than with my body.

She froze, her eyes, every bit of her focused on where my fingers wrapped around her hand and wrist.

"Maggie." The way I said her name felt like an incantation. I was being lured onto the dark side by my desire. In the moment, I didn't care about right and wrong. Couldn't care. There was only what my body wanted. It had been so long.

She drew an audible, ridiculously erotic breath. Then closed her eyes. I didn't know if she was steeling herself or giving in to desire. I didn't think. With the sea crashing beyond, the empty beach all ours, I pulled her to me again.

My arms scorched where I pressed against hers. The sensations drowned me. I let them wash over. It felt incredible. How could this be wrong? I inched my face to touch the apple of her cheek. Instinctively, I rubbed my jaw against her there. My breath shuddered. We gave in again, and this time she held onto the back of my head, grabbing as if her life depended on it. Mine certainly did.

"Oh God," she said.

That opened the floodgates. Our lips crushed against each other's, breathy, overwhelmed. She opened her mouth.

"Maggie," I whispered into her, then let my tongue slip inside, pulling her in closer, closer, all the way. "Oh, Maggie." I gripped at her hair, trying not to rip it out. My desire was so forceful, I had lost control.

I felt her hands on mine. Suddenly she was pulling away.

I tugged her lip between mine, then held on with my teeth. "Please."

She'd managed to put a metre between us. "No, don't. Please." Had her emotions scared her? Her eyes were glossy, her ribs rising and falling raggedly. "I can't go back there. I understand life isn't a fairy tale. I know the sacrifices soldiers make. You choose what's most important to you and you go for it."

Maggie's cheeks pinked, her chest heaved before her brain had a chance to work out she wasn't meant to show me any of that. She was angered by my peek behind the curtain. Which made me want to grab her behind her neck, pull her back to my lips. She began to yell, but I had begun imagining what it would be like, anticipating the touch of her lips, diving my tongue inside her mouth, deeper, deeper, pressing her into me. *Whoa.*

The way she said those words so articulately showed me how deeply I'd hurt her, how closely she held onto that justification for my actions. Like an apology would make all that go away. I was so dumb. If I really wanted this, the least I could do was find the right words to say so.

"Maggie or the world," she continued. "I'm not deluded enough to think I'm more important than saving lives."

"You are."

She spoke quickly as if she was terrified of what I'd said, too scared to believe it. "My whole life has been about those sacrifices. You don't need to say that. I'm a big girl. But I definitely don't want to talk about that."

"Is that how you think it went down? You've got it wrong. And that's my fault. I know that. And I will never let you feel like that again. I promise."

She looked so deeply into my eyes, searching, like she wanted to believe me but needed to find some physical evidence there.

While I had her attention, I continued. "I should never have considered the deployment. I should have chosen you without hesitation, because you are more important to me than any living soul on earth. What the fuck was wrong with me that I'd made that mistake? I've asked myself that so many times. I was a fucking moron."

She ignored the question, which we both knew was hypothetical. Hearing myself tell this story, I thought if I was this hopeless, perhaps I didn't deserve her. I would just fuck it up again, wouldn't I? The reality was worlds away from the fantasy of what it could be between us. That was what I'd forgotten.

The years of self-sufficiency hadn't left me unscathed, despite what I told myself. There had been hurt on both sides, walls erected to protect it, and that was not so easily undone. In fact, I wasn't so sure I had a clue how to be the man I'd promised myself I'd be if I ever got another chance with her. And then what? I would screw her over again? There was never anyone I had to dig this deeply for. It was new territory.

Even now, out of the gate, I was going too fast, despite the fact I'd planned to take it slow, make it easier on her because that's what she needed. If I didn't sort out my shit, that was going to prevent me from ever making things right. I straightened out, shook it off. Pretended to be unfazed by her silence for her benefit. Because what was there for her to say?

She wasn't ready. I shouldn't have said any of that yet. *I* wasn't ready for what she deserved. I'd gone too fucking fast. I was going to take a bad situation to nuclear if I kept up this pace. "Maybe things are moving too fast," I said.

She squinted, her eyes searching mine, unsure of my intentions, my words so out of sync with my body and everything I'd said before. My hand was clutching hers too tightly. I was probably crushing her fingers. I took the moment to look at her honestly, deeply. I hoped the look conveyed that I would do anything to get her back, but I wasn't sure what that was. I couldn't say that because if she thought I didn't know what I was doing, how could she ever trust me?

"You're right," she said, but I could see she was angry. She took it the wrong way, that I'd back out now that it all looked too hard.

"I'm sorry." I grabbed for her hand, but she pulled it away. God, I hated myself for being the one to make her suffer like that. There I was, the same hollow words spewing from my lips. Though I was determined to do whatever it took to make things right, that was becoming an increasingly impossible task.

To my surprise, she looked me in the eye and said, "I know you are." And that gave me hope. I nodded and grabbed her hand, this time too fast for her to pull away, so she'd know what that meant to me.

"Thank you," I said, gratitude singing inside me. One day, I'd tell her exactly what I should have done. No, I'd show her. For now, I'd say, "It was all my fault."

"No," she said, "it wasn't."

I wasn't going to shoot her words down, because I didn't know everything what was in her heart. Instead, we had a few blissful seconds of connection before she pulled away again.

"Look," I tried to focus on the practicalities before she ran off, which I sensed she was going to do, "why don't we concentrate on the most pressing issue—Flo. I'm going to tell her as soon as we get back."

"Look at us, treating Flo like a problem. It's so terrible. Thank you for telling her. And you're right. I can't hurt her in the way you're asking me to."

That's not exactly what I said. God, I really was going to fuck it up. "The way you *want* to."

"No. No!" She shook her head in a frenzied manner.

"She knows things aren't right between us. And she loves you deeply. She would never want you to throw away your chance at the real thing for her, when she knows she and I aren't meant to be . . . as much as it would hurt."

"Well, then why didn't she break it off with you?"

"Why didn't you break it off with Reg?"

"That's different."

"How?"

"You know, I forgot how incredibly irritating it is fighting with you. You always know you're right. So why even bother getting into it?"

She was right. I was a dick like that. But she made more reasonable points to persuade me to a different point of view than anyone I'd ever spoken to. And she was doing it again. Showing me my flaws. Most people were afraid to do that. It was always *Sir* this and *Sir* that.

Maggie continued. "I think it's best if we avoid any situations where we'll be forced to socialize. It's the beginning of the end of my friendship with Flo no matter what. A friendship can't survive such a giant betrayal. And no one's coming out a winner. You're right about that. You need to talk to Flo. Don't let things fall apart because of things left unsaid. Nothing works that way—no one wins."

That stung because I knew she was referencing our breakup. I got the sense she might have rested some of the responsibility of the silence that had been our relationship's death knell on herself after all this time. Neither of us were ready to get back into that just yet. I had to keep things simple.

"I am going to be clear on this. Nothing is happening between us." She got up and started to descend the rock.

So, what was that kiss? Was she actually ignoring the fact that it already had? And what about all that messaging? I bet she'd drawn some kind of line there. It would be like her to organize how she'd be illicit with me, and then shut down when anything beyond that occurred. God I loved her. And she loved me. I just had to trust, and make sure I kept things slow, the way she needed.

"We'll see," I called out, grabbing for her hand one last time, savoring the second before her fingertips fell away

She didn't turn back, but I could just feel the ends of her mouth being forced down to cover her fibber's smile. If she were still sitting here, I'd help her out with that, hold her in my arms and get us both prepared for the storm that was coming. And I knew where things would go from there. It would be so incredibly, overwhelmingly sensual if that kiss was any kind of indication. There was no stemming this tide. It was just a matter of trying to slow it down so it didn't kill us all in its wake.

SIXTEEN

MAGGIE

IT HAD BEEN difficult to concentrate on the afternoon work-shop, which Maggie knew they were particularly meant to focus on—Introducing Vegan Menu Options. The company had been getting customer feedback on the limitations of their vegan offerings and the higher ups had specifically hired this French professional to come and share his wealth of knowledge and experience with anyone who touched menu planning.

The chef was male and particularly good-looking with the kind of smirk that wasn't even attempting to hide his Casanova ways. He'd clearly taken a shine to Flo. Today, Flo had on a featherweight, floaty dress, and between that and Chef Martin's (three times he repeated the French pronunciation, even spelled it phonetically on the white board: Mar-*tahn*, emphasis on the *tahn*) impeccably groomed five-o'clock shadow and thick black hair, there was fire in the kitchen.

She wasn't surprised. Flo had a charming, engaging air and Maggie often saw men checking her out when they were out for drinks or lunch. She always said they were checking out Maggie, the thought of which made her smile.

Until she thought of her conversation on the beach with George.

She found herself wishing things could work out neatly. Flo running off with the Frenchman, telling Maggie she could see what was happening between George (Lionel) and her and she was just so happy they were all happy; *c'est la vie!*

That was never going to happen, but Flo seemed to encourage the handsy approach of Chef Mart*in*. The strange chemistry between them threw Maggie even further off her game than she'd been after her talk—and worse—kiss, fucking hot kiss, which she was still buzzing from—with George. She didn't need any more weight tugging her justice scale in the naughty direction, and yet here Flo was, openly flirting with *Le Chef* when she'd spent the better part of the morning trying to maintain her friend's honor. She told herself whatever Flo chose to or not to do with Martin didn't change a thing.

Still, afterward, she asked Flo what had been going on between her and Mar-*tahn*.

"I told you. George and I are not doing well. It felt good to be wanted. You know what that's like, don't you, Maggie?"

She seemed angry, or accusatory, Maggie was too guilt-laden to pick which. "You're right. I'm sorry. I shouldn't have said anything."

"Well, secrets are no good either, Maggie."

The flinch was beyond her control.

Thankfully, Reg showed up and she excused herself to go back to the hotel room for a rest before dinner.

NEEDLESS TO SAY, when Maggie returned to the perfectly organized hotel room, the tidiness and tight corners of the cleaners' impeccable work felt at odds with her relationship with Reg.

What was she doing here still with him? At least she could do one thing right.

"Things aren't working between us, Reg. I'm not happy. You're not happy." There. She was out with it.

She wasn't about to wait around for George to tell Flo. She and Reg needed to go their separate ways regardless of the George factor. The George reemergence may have unearthed the ugly truth of her relationship with Reg sooner than she was comfortable with, but it was a truth distinct from anything to do with George.

"What are you saying, Maggie?" He shook his hands so dramatically, she had to stop herself from calling him out on it.

"I'm saying I think we should end things between us."

"No. No! I know I'm not perfect, but you can't walk out on me because of that." Now with the pointing. Phase Three involved shouting. She braced herself.

"Reg, you've been completely absent. Even when you're around, it's like you're not with me. You're somewhere else. You've moved on already. It's just a matter of getting our lives caught up to where your head and heart are at. My head and heart too." Those last words had been the hardest to say.

"You're wrong. And why so suddenly are you confronting me about it?" He looked very upset in a way she hadn't been expecting. His chin quivered, and then he began to cry in loud snorts. "Flo hinted at something like this."

Flo? It was quite upsetting seeing him that way, his lips contorted, his body shaking. And it didn't help that she knew exactly why the things she'd been putting up with were suddenly unbearable—it *was* because of George. The comparison was too shocking. "It's not suddenly." *Lies.* But what would the truth do other than make the situation worse?

"Please, don't leave me. I know I haven't been the best to

you. But give me another chance. I need you right now, Maggie." He shouted the last bit.

Right now. The words jarred, despite the volume, and she couldn't bear to cause him further pain at the moment. She understood needing people. Shouldn't she just give him a little more time? She'd certainly used a fair portion of his.

"Come here," she said, and she let him cover her with his body, to hold onto her like a port in the storm. She owed him that at least. He'd done the same for her.

THEY'D FALLEN asleep like that. And when she woke in the dark two hours later to Reg's snore in her ear, it was nearly dinner time, and her right arm and leg were pins and needles. He was literally crushing her. She kept turning those words of Reg's over in her mind: *Flo hinted at something like this.* Had he merely put his own interpretation onto something benign she'd said? He was never one for sarcasm. Perhaps he'd simply misunderstood a joke? Either way, she couldn't make it sit well.

Anyway, there were bigger problems. She'd chickened out in breaking up with Reg. She told herself she *would* break things off soon, but that if he needed the extra time to get used to the idea, then it was the least she could do. He'd been a sufficient, if unreliable, life raft for her these couple years. If it was her turn to see him to shore, that was something she was capable of.

She didn't hate him. She just didn't want to be with him. And if selfishness was his weak point, she would go out of her way to make sure he couldn't say the same about her. There was only one night left of this conference. After that, she'd come up with a measured, long-tailed exit strategy he could deal with. Then a Flo strategy. Then a George strategy. Simple, right?

Following that she could move onto solving world hunger and finally settling into peace in the Middle East.

She lowered herself into a steamy bath filled with almond and fig bubble foam and tried to clear her mind, be present in the soothing cocoon of the moment in which she wasn't expected to face up to some horrible truth to the people she loved. Maggie closed her eyes and concentrated on her breathing, trying to focus on her third eye. She was no stranger to relaxation techniques. In a moment, her muscles began to drop, her jaw relaxed, and her arms felt heavy as she let them sink.

Then her phone's calendar jingled. She knew what it was without looking: dinner with Flo and George in one hour.

Sitting up, she reached over the side of the tub for her phone and texted Flo.

MAGGIE: *Reg and I need a quiet night in. We're going to get room service.*

FLO: *All okay?*

She couldn't lie anymore. It was too much lying.

MAGGIE: *Not great. But I'll talk to you about it another time.*

FLO: *xoxo*

Her chest felt like it was plummeting.

MAGGIE: *xoxo*

She inhaled a deep breath and submerged herself completely under the foamed water. For one whole minute she was able to hold her breath. Maggie emerged gasping, wondering what she was doing, trying to show herself she could block it all out?

Being unable to breathe was nothing compared to being unable to touch George the way she couldn't stop thinking of doing. God, his mouth on hers. She was still alight with the sensations of his touch yesterday on the beach, even while he was ordering his words to break the terrible reality to Flo.

After how broken she was post-George, now she was eager to neatly tie up the three obstacles, then dip right back into him. It was a terrible cyclone gathering speed, sure to flatten them all. There was no list where any of this could be crossed off, job done. And yet, she felt her mind gravitating to close the circuit exactly that way.

Then she sent another text. This time to George. Though she worried about the possibility of Flo seeing it, she also recalled George being a screener. He didn't let texts or calls happen to him. He used to dedicate a few minutes every few hours to addressing them, on his own schedule—no alerts, no distractions outside of that time. She gambled on the idea he still did the same.

MAGGIE: *George, don't tell her. We can't do this. Please don't pursue this.*

It had been impulsive, that text. And she sensed it had more to do with proving to herself that she could cross him off her list like anything else. As soon as she'd tapped SEND, she regretted it. She hadn't meant a word.

Even worse, when there was no answer, Maggie was left to interpret things on her own. Which left her unsure where things stood.

Instead of leaving things like that, she went in for another round.

MAGGIE: *Forget my text. Continue on as you said. Tell Flo. She needs to know. We need to be honest about our feelings for each other.*

Oh God, oh God. Was that even worse? For someone who had decided to sit the night out, she'd certainly put her foot in it. And that last sentence was open for interpretation. It could mean she needed to be honest about still being in love with him too. And she certainly hadn't been ready to say that. Now what power did she have left? Exactly none.

What had she done? Had fate given her one last chance and then she'd gone and kicked it in the teeth? That's how it felt. God, if she was afraid of being wrecked, then she needed to face facts: she already was. She had to go off the map and trust herself, and that was somewhere she'd been hesitating to go for a long time. But maybe those ridiculous messages were just that—acting on instinct. Messy, but getting there in the end?

Checking her phone constantly, Maggie was on tenterhooks all the way home the next morning, which thankfully, was not on the same flight as George and Flo, since Reg had to be back for an early meeting. He was so clingy on the plane, she felt like she couldn't breathe.

It didn't help that she kept picturing George punching in a text on his phone, Flo right alongside trying to catch a glimpse. Something along the lines of what he'd said at the beach, returning her declaration of love in writing, where she could look at it again and again.

But there was no text. In the lounge, rather than let the thought of bacon enter her mind, she avoided the breakfast buffet altogether, sticking with black coffee, telling herself that at least she was trying to keep her wits about her. But trying wasn't something she ever gave any great marks.

Instinct was one thing, but trying without a result was a fail in the military climate she'd grown up in. But she wasn't in that world any longer. Perhaps she needed a kick into gear. And wasn't that just what that final message was? She *was* trying. And it was messy. But once George read that second message about her feelings, following the first one, he'd know how deeply she'd had to dig down to say those words, to allow herself to look so weak. And he'd know that she truly meant them.

Maggie stood to get a second coffee, and as she did, she inhaled the smell of bacon deeply into her body.

SEVENTEEN

FLO

FIRST LET ME SAY THIS—I was jealous. And jealousy can make us do some terrible stuff that we wouldn't normally. I'd read that the green-eyed monster brings on spikes of activity in brain areas that deal with pair bonding and social rejection and pain, which made sense to me. I only did what I did because I knew all along that I was a rebound for Lionel's ex, Maggie.

The reason scientists studied the effects of jealousy on the brain in the first place was to work out why jealousy so often led to violence. At least, I didn't get to that point. But I'll be the first to admit, it all spiraled out of control.

I didn't want to hurt anyone. I just wanted to feel like I *mattered* in this scenario, that I wouldn't be shoved out, never to be given a second thought.

The idea of being a rebound! A rebound is by definition a distraction. So, if I was going to be that, I was going to really put on a show.

EIGHTEEN

GEORGE

MAGGIE'S WAFFLING about going through with things showed me that she was struggling to let me in again. I got it. I'd botched things up in the past. Big time. But the fact that she was so emotional that she hadn't taken the time to cool down, consider her course of action and stick with it, rather than impulsively broadcast whatever was on her mind proved that she wasn't pretending to be strong for my benefit. And that, folks, was what they call honesty, being your true self.

If I played my cards right, and remained patient, I could give her the Happily Ever After she deserved. But on the other hand, if it all took too long and gave her too much time to think, I could just as easily lose my chance.

GEORGE: *I love you. I am going to tell Flo tonight.*

It was a busy day at work and I don't do alerts on my phone, so I was surprised when I sat down in the afternoon to see she hadn't responded.

I told myself everyone misses text messages from time to time, even if this would be the one time in their life they'd be obsessively checking and tried again.

GEORGE: A lesser guy than myself might take the silence personally. But not me, obvs. xx

Oh God, why had I written that? The longer I waited for her reply, the more those words sounded like they came from some massive fuckwit. And guess who the massive fuckwit was?

On the walk back to my place after work, she still hadn't texted me, so I rang her mobile. There must have been something wrong because it didn't ring and gave no voicemail prompt. Fucking technology.

NINETEEN

MAGGIE

SHE COULD NOT FREAKING BELIEVE that George had not answered her text messages. Neither the first one calling things off nor the second one showing how overcome with emotion she was that she didn't even know what she was saying. The silence just gave her room to brood about how unguarded she'd allowed herself to be with him. Once again. God, she was a stupid, stupid girl. She deserved this.

She checked her phone incessantly. Nothing. Nothing. And fucking nothing again.

Still, it was too early not to give him the benefit of the doubt. Anything could have happened, right? It could have been a matter of national security for crying out loud, and here she was concerned about a text! They'd laugh about it later, surely.

But later came and nothing.

Her focus wavered as she washed her hair, tried to scrub last night from her cheekbones. Why in fuck had she not heard from George? This was so ridiculous. They were in the 21st century. People did not have communication issues like this.

George didn't do social media because of his military reputation. She knew from her father's lectures that it was dangerous to plot out anything about where you spent your time, who you spent it with, and what you were going to do in the future.

There were people against what the military was doing in all parts of the world and it wasn't difficult for them to work out where a picture was taken, that you worked at a specific building, who you loved, or which street you lived on. And there was nothing stopping any of those people from hurting you by targeting your friends and family either.

Sure, George had a Facebook profile, but it hadn't been updated for nearly a decade. And it had his residence as Tallahassee, which was his idea of a joke. Everywhere else George was a ghost.

The sun went down, she showered, checked her phone, ate, checked her phone, endured fifteen minutes of arm caresses from Reg even though she'd told him dozens of times the feel of such rubbing made her skin crawl, and told herself she was doing the right thing giving Reg a bit more time to get used to her leaving. That George would understand why she was still sitting here binge watching yet another crime series on Netflix and picking at Vietnamese takeout that Reg had surprised her with (including all the dishes he liked and none she did, in fact, one—octopus—she despised). Maggie kept grabbing for her phone.

"Should I be jealous?" Reg asked. "Who you looking to hear from?"

His curiosity, despite its edge of disbelief someone could ever be after her, was at least an improvement to the sexting day when he'd caught her photographing herself basically pornographically and hadn't so much as batted an eyelash.

Hopefully he wouldn't want to have sex because she just couldn't bring herself to go there. And there were only so many nights she'd be able to lean on headaches for get-out-of-bed-free cards.

While she tried to ignore the nails on the chalkboard feel of Reg's fingers on her arm and the intrusive pressure and odor of repeating Octopus with Nuoc Chaum, she took a stroll through the emotional history that had brought her to this particular juncture,

So far, relationships in her life had been the result of what she needed at the time. All she had to do was turn her head for evidence of that. Of course, she'd lived an itinerant life as the child of an army officer. And once her mother died, her father seemed to put less and less importance on place.

He quietly began a relationship with a woman who'd been in and out of the periphery of their military social circle for as long as Maggie could remember, Jessica O'Rourke. But he never announced it to her, never asked how she felt. And she forgave him that. What would the point have been?

She felt like her mother was dead and it was totally fucking weird that this woman who'd once made small talk with her lovely, quiet *Mumsy*, as Maggie used to jokingly call her, about training bra shopping was now sleeping on her mother's painstakingly ironed sheets, which were unironed now, of course, because Jessica is quite down to earth, which Maggie can't pretend not to like. Besides, if Jessica didn't lay beside him, her father would be alone. That was just the reality.

Of course, Maggie wasn't in the house any longer. Her father had quite rightfully sent her to a boarding school in the ninth grade to save her the pain of endlessly switching schools. She hadn't been good at it, the transition growing that much harder each time so that by the time she was in the seventh grade, she'd stopped trying to make friends.

Of course, that meant the friends—and the boys—flocked to her standoffishness. But they weren't the friends she'd want. She didn't want any. In fact, she didn't want anything she'd miss if it would die, or if she'd have to leave.

Apparently, there were people who could get through this continual relocating with a modicum of charisma. They grew more and more outgoing and engaging and could grow up to be talk show hosts or artillery officers.

But Maggie suspected they were full of shit. That they didn't trust any of the people they surrounded themselves with, and kept a bag packed to escape at the drop of a hat.

At least she was honest. Coupling seemed to happen without her realizing it.

But then she'd met George. And she'd allowed herself to be seduced by the intensity of her feelings, by how *big* their relationship felt in comparison to anything else she'd experienced. She was pretty sure this was it. But what would she know? Rather than try to pin it down, which she'd found to be impossible, she made endless lists of pros and cons of emigrating to Australia, which in the end couldn't help her decide.

So when he sat her down, his mountain of paperwork for repatriating at the ready, and asked, tenderly, his hand at her neck, "You coming with me?"

She'd nodded. "Yes." She swallowed. The words were as big as their relationship and she had trouble getting them out. "Yes!" she'd shouted the second time, because she wanted it to be experienced by George at the same scale.

He'd pulled her to him, and the urgency and sensitivity of her body's reaction underlined how right her decision had been. Who walked away from love like this just because it happened to be geographically ridiculous? She didn't sit down and say, *no, I'm too afraid of people I love leaving me and so I'm making this decision in the wrong frame of mind.* This was not the simplistic way her mind worked.

She floated along with his plan and waited for the shoe to

drop. Because it would. So what was the point of worrying about it? She'd deal with it when the time came.

And two years later, on one of those incredible clear Sydney nights, it did. At least she'd give George this: he was a man about it. Sat her down and said, "This isn't working. You aren't happy. You have shut me out. And if you're going to do that, it's never going to work."

He was right, of course. All that flowing along with George had scared her stiff. Nothing could be this good and last. She'd turned into those "well-adjusted" military kids with her bag packed. And she hadn't even realized. And in the end, she couldn't be honest with him about it. Because it made her whole life feel like a sham.

She had no idea how to have relationships with people, and this was the one thing that was meant to be instinctive. Humans were social animals. They needed people. But she didn't know how to. And she wasn't about to admit that. He'd decided to go, she told herself, despite her own words, because that fit the narrative better.

And then came Reg. And he didn't delve deeply enough to work out any of that. It was never going to work with him and that was what made it work for her at the time. He was a life raft. She forgave him his shitty treatment of her because she deserved it. She wasn't with him for the right reasons.

She'd always thought George would come back in a day, a week, a month, a year, and say, "I was just away to show you that you do need me, that you *can* let me in if not doing so means we can't work."

But he never did. She'd told that to Flo one drunken night before George was Lionel. This confession took place on the same night she'd told her about that time she'd kissed another guy, nearly slept with him, right before she and George broke up. Back when the world still offered some promise of sense, even if she hadn't quite cracked the code.

That was the only time she'd ever bared so much to another living person. And God love her, Flo only said, "Oh, Mags, who doesn't have secrets?" and had never brought it up again. Who would have thought they were in love with the same man?

TWENTY

FLO

YOU WOULD THINK it would take more than blocked text messages to prevent fate. But Maggie and George didn't make contact with each other after her final text giving him the go-ahead to break the big news to me. I made sure they couldn't get through to the other's phones. Once they'd decided they were going to move forward, they needed another obstacle. The phone thing was perfect.

It saddened me that day after day they took what appeared to be a mutual silence at face value. Perhaps there was no such thing as true love. I felt the blocks were the right way to help them along, by throwing a few difficulties along the path to love to make the whole thing more romantic.

In the end, when they finally get together, they'll probably appreciate it more because they'd almost let their chance slip through their fingers. I could just tell them but stepping in so blatantly seemed to muddy the ideas of fate and destiny that played such a key role in the picture I held dear. Surely, they'd find a way. I had to have hope. After all, wasn't my anxiousness on their behalf proof of how well their story was going?

I felt sure it was a stroke of genius, blocking Maggie and George (I've started calling him that now because that's who Maggie knows him as) from each other's phones.

George's was simple. I just did it when he was in the shower. Maggie's was a bit trickier. But as soon as I saw Maggie's text message on George's phone saying he should go ahead, I knew I had to act fast.

I told George I was running down to the shop to grab something for dinner, and instead grabbed an Uber to Maggie's. I'd swiped her work I.D. at the last session with Chef Martin, and now I knocked on her door as the savior realizing I'd accidentally walked off with her pass.

"Oh thank God, Flo. I would have never been able to get into the building tomorrow! Let me make you a cuppa!"

"No problem, tea sounds good. Can I borrow your phone for a second to check something online? I left mine at home. Duh."

"Sure." She thumbed her phone to unlock it and handed it over. Without a second thought, she left me to my fake Google task and made her way to the kitchen to put the kettle on. It was cute how she drank T2 Melbourne Breakfast just like George.

"Just need to use your toilet," I said. I took the phone with me. She didn't notice. Or didn't say anything if she thought I was surfing the net on the toilet, which is pretty gross, but whatever.

I scrolled through her text message history. I was a bit shocked to see the nearly naked photo of her backside, and I had to give it to them, they'd been creative with their methods of getting around physically doing the wrong thing. A shock of jealousy blasted through me. I wanted this for them, but it also hurt that I didn't have this for myself. Would I ever?

I told myself to get back to the mission at hand. Maggie hadn't received any new messages from George since she'd given the go-ahead. Minutes later, I reemerged and the block was done. It was that simple.

I was not cold-hearted. It hurt to do this to someone I'd come to love. For I had grown to care deeply for Maggie. That was the part I hadn't expected. I'd been jealous with rage in the beginning, which was how I'd become a chef and come to study *Five Meals, Done!* and Maggie's culinary style—get super-excited about new ingredients, overdose them in everything, move onto the next—so intensely that I knew I'd nail the interview.

But there was a point a couple of months into my new job where everything—besides George, of course—had clicked into place. I loved the job. I loved Maggie. I was self-sufficient and even toyed with the idea of breaking it off with George and pretending I'd never done any of that other stuff.

When I thought about how far I'd gone, I was mortified. This wasn't the way I was used to behaving. But there was something about them that obsessed me. They belonged together. And playing a part in that made me feel touched by their love, like some of it might rub off on me.

I'd never had a serious relationship before. Men had flitted in and out of my life. I knew I was pretty and could mold myself to any situation to make people like me. I didn't seem to have trouble meeting them. But neither did I ever feel the earth orbited around them. Nearly everyone I'd known since grade six had felt that way—just fine. What was wrong with me? Was I missing the bit that became entangled in such a thing?

When George became the most recent perfect-on-paper man to enter and—I could already see from early on—immi-nently leave my life, I came upon a photo of the two of them on the Manly ferry so ridiculously lost in each other. I vowed to work out what made a couple like that tick.

I wanted this ache George and Maggie had for each other.

That photo of them on the ferry. Their love was screaming off the image. The way I felt looking at that was the closest thing to aching for love I ever had.

They were each incredible, layered people. Strong. Much stronger than most people try and fail to be. Must be a military thing, I thought, beginning to forge my list of what made love click. Self-sufficient and a complete package with or without a partner.

That was certainly something for the list, something deficient in me, and if I was honest, something that was probably standing in my way of love. Here I was walking around feeling like a half that could never be complete, a toy waiting for someone to play with in just that right way.

At first, I tucked the picture deep inside one of my storage boxes in the closet. But it was so inconvenient to keep coming up with excuses for digging in there, I told myself it was better to carry it in my purse. But then I began looking at it daily. Like I had to get my dose of that feeling before I started my day. Just to taste the possibilities.

And that was probably where the problems really began. She began to feel like a real, live part of our relationship. Always there. Between us. I felt like I knew her. And then one day it hit me. I had to. I'd find her.

I hadn't thought much past that. By then, George and I were merely coexisting, roommates enjoying the ease of shared rent and someone to split the chores with. We had sex twice a week like parents of young children rather than a young couple in the honeymoon phase of a relationship.

I could see he was picturing her the whole time. Sometimes that got me off. And I sensed that me acting all Maggie, even if he didn't know it, made things last longer than it would have otherwise. I sussed out every detail of her I could find. On social media, it wasn't too hard. She was a chef. In a matter of minutes,

I could find myself warming to the career. I loved food, the lovely aromas, fresh herbs and veggies. Yes, I'd be a wonderful chef.

I'd liked George. A lot. He experienced life on such a deeper level than most people did. He understood more deeply, felt more deeply, enjoyed more deeply. But I could tell there was something unattainable about him.

I wanted, needed, to know what it was. But I could see how stupid that was now. If someone didn't want you, it didn't matter why. It didn't mean there was something deficient about you either. It amounts to chemistry. Still, he hadn't even given me his actual name!

The bits of you that felt jagged up against his bits. And there were jagged bits. Most often when he was feeling and doing and understanding so deeply, I watched him, not being brought in to get the same high.

We were different. And not the kind of different that complimented the other. The kind of different that carved out two separate lives and then tried to overlap them when it felt right to do so. It wasn't great—us together, though individually, I think we are extraordinary.

Finding out who *did* fit snugly and perfectly alongside him was not purposeful. But when I came across the photo of the two of them, and I saw the look someone had captured in his eye looking at her when she hadn't seen him watching. Wow. That blew me away. He loved her. Any idiot could see it.

And in real life, I came to admire and enjoy my time with both of them. While I felt I didn't fit with George, I felt I *did* fit with Maggie. It was different with female friendships. You could be honest with each other. You could just say whatever you were thinking and they seemed to always understand where you were coming from, instead of taking it personally the way a man would. You never had to say "It's not about you" to your best girlfriend. They already knew that.

Sometimes I thought Maggie was my other half. That with her, I *was* complete. And I sensed this self-containment would help me get to a point where I could be in love with a man. That feeling and my relationship to the love between George and Maggie began to merge in a strange, messy way.

It all became larger than I could comprehend. But I knew this—it felt great. I loved Maggie. And the more I began to love Maggie, the more I wanted her to be with George. They were meant to be. It was a no-brainer. But I never felt ready to let them go. How many times had I said we were busy and couldn't meet her and Reg for dinner? Lots.

But then the time was right. I could sense it deep in my bones. And we had that dinner, and George and Maggie had their meeting. It was perfect. The look on her face, the reaction George tried to stem, the way he'd risked it and followed her to the bathroom. Gorgeous. The way the picture made me feel times one million. The love energy was everywhere. I was swept away in it. Perhaps that's why I felt slightly more generous to Reg than he deserved. That *crostino* comment! Jesus.

And then after, I stopped Maggie from coming out with her confession more than once. It would have been too easy getting it all out so quickly.

I felt bad, knowing the turmoil she must have experienced, but at the same time, I knew they needed the conflict to get it right this time. But there was something else. The closer they got to getting back together, I began to feel betrayed by Maggie, the person who had completed *me*.

How could she keep this from me? *But you're keeping a big secret yourself.* I knew that, but still. I couldn't quite let her go, and the two of them back together meant the end of that special friendship Maggie and I had.

I sensed this sharply. And no matter how I tried to argue myself out of the stance, every action I took seemed to keep their reunion from happening. At any cost. Was my meddling in pursuit of something more than an exciting road to happily ever after? I told myself it wasn't. Because in the end, didn't I really want them to have their wedding bells and life of bliss?

I'D BEEN ALL SET to tell Flo the entire truth when she came home, but all she could talk about was Maggie and that fucker Reg, how he'd been cheating and now things were finally called off.

I was so fucking pissed.

That fucker.

I had to remind myself I would go to jail if I killed him. It didn't seem like such a large price to pay for wiping him from Maggie's life.

Of course, he was cheating on her. Women with their incredible ability to reason away the obvious. It was manipulation of someone with a beautiful heart. It was using a person—one who mattered more to me than anything on this planet—as if she didn't mean a thing. I'd seen enough of that in my life to recognize it. Dick. I tried to unfurl my fists.

According to Flo, I wasn't meant to know this information.

"If Maggie knew I told you, she would be furious," Flo said. "She values our friendship so deeply."

"And you don't?"

"Oh, of course I do! It's just, Maggie's always had these

hang-ups about trusting people. It's a big deal she's let me in. Apparently her ex-boyfriend did a real number on her."

I had to get out of there. Immediately. I was just about to say so when Flo spoke over me.

"I THINK she should work through it with him, don't you?" she asked, looking inquisitive. Flo could pout like nobody else, and she did it then to perfection. Why did that strike me as manipulative?

"What do I know? I don't even know the guy. From what I do know, he's a douche, but I'm certainly in no place to know what Maggie wants." I'd blurted out too much. It was uncharacteristic. Flo smiled hugely, as if I'd said something hilarious. Did she *know*?

Also, had Maggie told Flo this thing about Reg so that it *would* get back to me? The more I thought about it, the more that seemed likely. Even if it was subconscious on her part, she might be sending me a message. This was ridiculous. I sounded like a girl. But I also wasn't taking any chances either way. I was going to her place. I could have The Talk with Flo another night. If Maggie needed me, this time I was damned well going to be there.

I stood and walked to the window. "I'm going for a run," I said, and started to tug at my buttons.

"Another run?" Flo asked, ducking back through the bedroom with her plaid nighty on. "Should I start to worry that *you're* cheating?"

I tried for a nonchalant laugh but didn't think I quite pulled it off. What I said instead wasn't much better, "I know you deserve better."

She didn't question me, and I didn't wait around to invite

her to. I closed myself in the bedroom, yanked off my cams, showered quickly, and pulled on my running gear.

God, I was in some serious shit. Was I any different than Reg? Of course, I was. I hadn't done anything. Well, not what I wanted to do anyway. And I wouldn't until we were free to be together. I was a person with morals. I had a code and it was instinctive. I didn't explain it away in the manner Reg was likely doing.

Somehow, he'd make this out to be Maggie's fault. Of course, he had. The fists again. I closed my eyes and breathed. I wasn't going to let my temper get this situation into an even messier spot.

I walked a block, telling myself it was a warm-up. But when I turned onto Oxford Street, I stopped at the light and just stood on the corner instead of crossing to my regular running route. Maggie's apartment was a ten-minute run from here. I made it in seven.

I couldn't stop picturing her chastising herself because she hadn't cared enough not to be with someone like Reg, because she didn't want to leave herself open to be hurt again, the way she'd been hurt by me. This way, at least, she'd have told herself, she was safe. And that was my fucking fault.

TWENTY-TWO

MAGGIE

SHE CAME AS FAR as walking to George's part of town, but then she began to panic. How had she gotten here? Maggie had been expecting to hear from George and she hadn't. She couldn't get him on the phone. Every time she tried to ring his mobile nothing happened—no ring, no voicemail, no error message. What the fuck?

Now literally all she did was think about him and her in the city as if they were the only people there. It seemed impossible she hadn't run into him, hadn't seen him since Noosa when the two of them loomed so large in her heart. But this was all emotional urgency, skewing reality. She understood that. And yet, there was something not quite right about his silence.

Last night, Reg had woken her from a dream in which he said she'd been screaming *More! More! Yes!*

"I must have been good," Reg said, which she thought was rich, since they hadn't had sex in weeks.

You'll never be as good as George in or out of that dream, she thought, and her face had gone so red she had to turn away.

But all of that was still under her control. Once the truth

was out, it wouldn't be. That's what kept her knuckles from knocking on George's door. Until now.

Now here she was, a block over from his place, reaching the corner unsure in which direction she'd turn—toward him or away. What was that saying she loved from Geena Davis? "If you risk nothing, then you risk everything." She'd happened upon it on Pinterest one day and it had struck her.

If he was going to tell Flo, she wanted to be there for him. Everything was risked, and going to his apartment right now, knocking on the door when Flo would most likely be there, struck her as the perfect statement of putting it all on the line for him. She was not afraid, the move said. And it was important they both understood that.

As she turned the corner onto George and Flo's uphill cobblestone street, Maggie's throat felt like it was closing up. She envisaged Geena Davis. Yes, she had great hair, but she was in *Thelma and Louise*, and she was in a convertible, driving off a cliff.

But that was a film about two women who let life make all their decisions until they couldn't take it anymore. And here she was telling life she wasn't going to live that way anymore.

Sure, Maggie was grasping at straws for something to assure her she was doing the right thing. But such assurances didn't exist. She cleared her throat loudly so that two people turned around, but she kept going. Until she was at Flo and George's door.

TWENTY-THREE

FLO

I WAS GETTING VERY good at this. I watched Maggie cross the street on cue to our place just as I'd basically sent George to Maggie's place to help her through the fake cheating Reg issue I'd invented.

No, I didn't go so far as to put a tracker on her phone. I wasn't a *psycho,* and somehow that was where psycho territory began, I'd told myself. I'd seen enough BBC miniseries about scorned lovers to know that when the victim entered stalking territory was when you started to change your loyalties to the cheater's side.

Still, I wouldn't mind being that *Dr. Foster* from my most recent series binge. She had some serious balls—whether she'd gone off the rails or not--and she was sexy and carried herself with an enviable dignity to boot.

I was expecting Maggie because George had texted her two days ago, but she'd not received the response because of the mutual blocks I'd placed on their phones. She'd be going nuts now. She was so distracted at work today, I picked up the slack for her, doing most of our shared work. "Thanks, Flo," she said. "I don't know why I'm so hopeless today."

But *I* knew why. And I knew *her, loved* her, which is why I was the only person in the world who could do this wonderful thing for her. *I hope she appreciates it,* I thought, and then shook it off. I was expecting her.

The frisson of satisfaction I had at seeing her down there on my street, according to plan, was chilling. There was so much pleasure in a job well done. Maggie was a decent person, a truly good person, and that was why my heart went out to her as she looked back and forth—toward our place and away.

Despite the hopes for the future, she was gutted about all this. My lovely friend. Who had ever cared for me the way Maggie did? No wonder all these men couldn't let her go. She had a way of letting you know how special you were to her, how rare these deep connections were. Maggie truly treasured the people she loved. And that *made* us treasures. Even now, I could feel my spine straighten at the idea of her out there, struggling between the love of her life and her best friend.

I smiled proudly as she made her decision, as I knew she would. I'd set it up perfectly. She was coming after him. I knew she wouldn't let life career her along in its current when she was given this second chance. By me.

I watched her approach the building, then made myself a cup of tea from the recently boiled kettle, spilled half out as if I'd been sitting around drinking the tea and worrying all this time.

I wasn't going to make it *easy* for her. Everyone knows as things come to a climax, true love is at its most vulnerable. It could go either way at this point and that's what made it so valued and treasured at the happy ending. When the bell rang, I answered in a startled voice. "Hello? Who is it?" I might even get an Oscar for this performance. I was a natural.

"It's Maggie. Can you let me up, please?"

Her tone was restrained. One that placed miles between us.

I hadn't been prepared for that. Why hadn't I realized? Of course, I'd never be a glorious hero, would I? I'd be the victim. The reminder of their wrong doings. It would be too awkward.

But once I was settled in with Reg, and everyone saw things were as they were meant to be, we'd all be fine. Time healed all; wasn't that the saying?

Though I heard Maggie's footsteps up the stairs, I waited for her to knock before I got out of my seat. I sniffed loudly, as if I was trying to control some intense crying, then said, "One minute," so she'd think I was trying to calm myself enough to open the door.

When I swung the door open and she caught sight of how distraught I looked, I saw her determination drain right out of her. Her shoulders dropped, she audibly sighed, then caught herself, dragged her mouth into a sympathetic smile. "What's wrong, Flo?" She swallowed big, and I knew she was thinking, *This is it. He's told her.*

"Oh, Maggie!" I threw my arms around her in the doorway. The cries that came were not faked. I knew the friendship was dying and I was gutted. Maggie hugged me back. She was an excellent hugger, and I breathed in the clean, slightly floral scent of her beautiful, shiny red hair. My wonderful Maggie.

When our arms unwound, she held me by the hand and led me inside, closed the door and sat down, knee to knee on my blue velvet couch. Maybe the victim wasn't the absolute worst. There was a wonderful tenderness to this treatment.

"I know what's wrong, Flo."

I quirked my head in surprise. "You do?"

"I do. And I hate that you were in the dark about it."

"But how do you know?" I had to cut her off quickly. Otherwise she'd be out with it. And there was more suffering she had to do before she got back with George. Otherwise it would be all wrong. "Mother's doctor only just phoned me a half hour ago."

Maggie's face cycled through about ten expressions—shock, confusion, concern, anxiety, regret, relief, empathy. "Your mother's doctor? What happened?"

I gave her the rundown. Mother would have her carotid artery procedure the following day, I told her. Two days in the hospital, then my brother would take over the care so I could return to work. Even though Mom would be unkind to him the whole time, punishing him for the sins of their father, though he'd been right there alongside me, hiding under the blankets when tempers flared. George always liked my brother. Bonded over being the hated males. I was so moved, I nearly believed the whole thing.

"Is George coming home now, to be with you, to go with you to your mother?"

"He's out for a run. He doesn't know yet. I can't seem to get him on his phone."

One of her eyebrows raised. This was hopeful. If he was having technical difficulties, then he may have told me about their secret history. But she couldn't be sure. And she was too kind and thoughtful to bring it up now.

"Well, do you know where he runs? Maybe I can find him for you."

"Oh, Maggie, I don't know where he goes. We aren't so close these days, like I told you. Who knows if he's even running?" I probably took it a bit too far there. It was difficult to stay on point. Part of me was jealous. The jealousy made me veer off course, let my emotions steer me.

"Well, here's what we're going to do. We're going to book you on a flight to Townsville, get you packed, and then I'm going to find George while you rest up. Your mother's going to need you."

I nodded. I didn't trust myself to speak.

"Do you want George to go with you?"

I shook my head, looked down, as if there was more on my mind I wasn't saying. I nailed it.

Maggie squeezed my hands in hers. "Leave it with me," she said.

Maggie made good on her word and after she tucked me tenderly in bed, locked up and descended the stairs, I made my way to the window and watched as she paced back and forth waiting for an Uber ride to pick her up outside my building. She knew exactly where she was going, didn't she?

And she'd surprise him, just when he'd been to her place to defend her honor, probably knocked Reg on his ass, which I'd be there to soothe (hee-hee), and he'd think, *yes, this is destiny.* God, I was good.

TWENTY-FOUR

MAGGIE

"BE a bit of traffic up to Coogee, right now, Love." The driver was grandfatherly and kept saying soothing things about the jam all the way to the beach town where she and George had begun their Australian history. She was gambling anyway. Did she really think she'd know just where he'd go to find her and that they'd both be there at the same time? Maybe he was just having a run after all.

But Maggie's instinct was right. She watched him play with the beermat incessantly. He looked for her from the other entrance, so she had a second to observe him searching for her. Incredible that they'd both come here to see each other at the same time. George was in his running gear. She loved that it was the same stuff he'd worn when they were together. She'd even been with him when he picked out those black shorts with the zipper pocket for keys and the inside pouch for his debit card.

But despite the fact she had ostensibly come here on Flo's behalf, now she was here, on their old turf, just the two of them, she felt like she was crossing a new line. And if she let herself get here, she sensed there wasn't much she wouldn't do. It was his silence that made her desperate.

When she hadn't heard from him, she thought she'd lost her chance with him. Again. And that resonated so deeply as a mistake that it felt worse than any of the other worries she'd been battling—red lines and such. That had to mean something.

Seeing him now, anxious to locate her, showing a weakness she'd never seen in him, made her feel closer to him than ever. As if now, finally, she could trust that he was ready to bare all and be what she needed. And she could tell that scared him. But he was doing it anyway and that meant the world.

She'd been spotted. He froze, his gaze unwavering. A dense clutch of past, present, and yes, even future, connected them across the musty, oddly silent room. The absence of music made the moment go on forever and lent it the gravity it deserved. Who in this life was lucky enough for a second chance? In a way, it was Flo who had brought them to this moment. Such a strange mix of emotions welled inside her.

Her exhale rattled her chest. Even while she was here to deliver the news of Flo's ill mother, she was consumed with her overwhelming desire for George. If he would have her, she would take up where he'd left her, his lips on hers at the beach.

He smiled and she began to cross the large dining area to the classic mahogany and bronze bar. She'd once thought of him while she sat at the table she just walked past, eating fish and chips one night with Reg, thought how he would order a Tooey's New if he was there, how he'd get her a glass of bubbles before she even realized. She'd been shoulder hopping that whole night, looking for George without admitting it to herself.

That fantasy was here along with the real George, who, by the time she reached his place at the bar, was grabbing for her elbow. He pulled her before his chair, tucked her between his splayed knees, and buried his face in her hair.

She felt faint from his breath there. Maggie closed her eyes and drank in the sensations, his hand now clutching her thigh. "Maggie," he said into her ear. She felt a thud at her core.

"I have to tell you something," they both said synchronously, and turned face to face.

"You go first," he said, twirling a strand of her hair in his fingers.

"Okay," she said. "I am so glad to see you here. I knew you'd be here. I went to your place and Flo said you were out running, and I knew you'd be here. And here you are."

"You came to see me?"

"Yes, because I didn't hear from you on text and I couldn't get you on the phone."

"What do you mean? I didn't hear from *you*. Wait. Wait! Give me your phone."

She thumbed to unlock it and passed it over. George scrolled through to his number, which incredibly still had a photo of the two of them together on it.

He saw the picture. "That day on the Manly Ferry." He enlarged it and looked at it for a long while. Then he pulled her in close and pressed his lips to hers. Shivers ran up the backs of her arms. She trembled as he nudged her open with her tongue.

Slowly he pulled away, rubbed at her hair and smiled as if to say, *Oh, there you are, finally, where you belong.* "I thought *I* had that photo. Been looking for it everywhere."

"You do have it. I made you a copy for your birthday."

He shook his head, then touched his name on the screen, put the call on speaker so we could both hear. It was the same nothing I was getting whenever I tried his phone. I said as much.

George backed up into the settings menu and tapped the phone icon. Next, he chose "blocked numbers," which I never even knew existed. There he was.

"I never did that," I said.

George didn't speak, just raised a finger as he went through the same process on his own phone, to find I was blocked there.

"Who would do that? I asked.

"Well, there's only two people I can think of, and one of them I just punched in the face."

"Oh no, Reg? Why?"

"Because he's cheating on you."

"What? No, he isn't. Not that I know of anyway."

"Hang on. Didn't you tell Flo today that Reg was cheating on you?"

She shook her head.

George furrowed his brow, then his sparkling blue eyes popped to a conclusion. "Then it must be Flo who did this to our phones. Think about it. She has access to mine all the time. No one else does. Did she have yours at any time on the day after the conference?"

Maggie thought back to Flo's surprise visit, her request for Maggie's phone. And how Flo had saved the day by returning her work pass. Had she orchestrated that? No. That couldn't be right. But it seemed to make sense. "Yes, she did. So what does this mean?"

"Well, I think it's safe to say she knows about us. And she doesn't appear to be happy."

Maggie dropped her head in her hands. From there she asked, "Did you really punch Reg in the face?"

"Of course, I did. No one cheats on you. And I'm not sorry. There are plenty of other reasons he deserves to be punched in the face. In fact, everything he's ever said to me has translated as an invitation to be punched in the face. *Crostinos*," he imitated.

She smirked.

"So, you didn't tell her?"

"I sat her down to and she literally placed her finger on my lips to stop me speaking and told me about Reg cheating on you.

All I could think was that I had to get out of the house and make sure you were okay. Instead, I wound up clocking Reg."

"Well, while you were doing that, I was at your place. And I was about to tell her, because I hadn't heard from you, and I felt like this was what I needed to do—for *us*." It felt strange and wonderful to say that word, and George's eyes smiled, a beautiful web of crinkles around the edges that broadcast happiness.

"But she stopped me too. But this time she had a very good reason. Her mother is sick. I booked her a flight to Brisbane. She's going in the morning. So even if it is Flo behind this phone blocking, I don't think now's the time to approach her about it."

"How do you know for sure her mother is sick?"

"Oh, George, surely you're not insinuating that she'd just make that up! Why?"

"I guess you're right. It's just that phone thing is seriously fucked up."

"Is it possible it wasn't her? That it was, I don't know, some kind of cyber-attack thing?"

"Why would somebody do that? How would they specifically choose to target you and me?"

It did sound ridiculous when he put it that way.

"Let's just look at what we know for sure. Our numbers were blocked in each other's phones. Flo made up some lies about Reg cheating on you and told me right when I was about to tell her about you and me. And then her mother was conveniently sent to hospital exactly when *you* were going to tell her. She knows."

"She knows." Maggie nodded, letting her shoulders fall. "Maybe Kimberly Prott tipped her off?"

He shook his head, as if to rid himself of the ridiculousness. "You know what I think?"

"What's that?"

"I think that Flo is going to be away tomorrow—even if she's making up this thing about her mum, which I'm pretty sure she is. Her mum is such a mean old thing, she'll live forever, killing everyone else around her in the process. And Reg is clearly not going to be up for much." George's eyes twinkled with anticipation. "Wait a minute. Speaking of Reg, weren't you meant to break up with him?"

"I know. I know! I'm hopeless. He begged me to stay and I gave in. Just to give him a bit more time to get used to it."

"Maggie."

"I know. Didn't I say I know?"

"Come here. You were saying, before I so rudely interrupted you." He pulled her between his legs. She nudged her pulsating center toward him, rubbed against where his shorts were stretched taut.

"Yes. I was going to say that I can't wait anymore. Fuck it. Fuck it all. Let's you and me go somewhere we can be alone," she said. "I need you."

"Oh, I love that idea. And I love hearing you say it. It means the world to me that you trust me enough to say those words." The pressure behind his shorts intensified on her thigh. He was on board.

"Maggie, I love you."

"I love you too," she said, closing her eyes, savoring the feel of him pulling her closer. He quieted and let his tongue and lips prove his words, bond them. And oh boy, did they.

This was it. It was going to happen. She felt herself gush as she leaned into his hardness.

She leaned in and poured all her desire into a kiss. Ages later, they came up for air.

"Okay, we've waited long enough," he said. "Why don't we go to Coogee together tomorrow? Our spot?" He tipped his chin at the beach beyond. "I'll pick you up at your place."

She nodded.

"But first, I'm walking you home. I want to make sure Reg is not going to give you a hard time."

"Unnecessary. He's probably already scared to death and wondering what the hell you care about it. I don't think it would be very nice for you to be there when I explained your vested interest."

"But it would be so much fun."

"Stop it."

"I don't like it, but you're a big girl. I trust your instincts. If you say you'll be safe with him, I believe you. But I might wait down the block for a few hours just in case."

I SLEPT ON THE SOFA. The next morning, I sipped my coffee silently. The tension between us was palpable. I wasn't meant to know Flo had lied about Reg cheating, but between that deception and the mobile blockings she'd orchestrated, I was feeling pretty damned angry. I still sensed this "illness" of her mother's was impeccably timed and didn't believe we'd scratched the surface of Flo's duplicity.

I managed to hold my tongue while I dropped Flo off at the airport. Besides, I was going to spend the day with Maggie. Nothing was going to get me down with that on the horizon.

"Listen, Lionel," she said, "I know you're here for me. The fact that you would offer to drop everything to come to support me, even when things haven't been exactly perfect between us, means a lot. But I want you to complete your training. And my mother would prefer to have me to herself. She's always been unwilling to share me. She'd see your presence as an intrusion." And I'd certainly never given the impression that I was going to accompany her.

She knew. I knew. She knew that I knew. What exactly were we playing at, pretending otherwise? Part of me was simply thinking, hey, this way, I get to have Maggie all to myself today. Why rock the boat? The other trained part of me was flashing warning! Warning!

In the silence of the car, I remembered how little Flo's mother would speak to me when we went there for Easter last year. She hated men, Flo had explained. Because her own father had been a bully, and she never quite forgave the opposite sex for his behavior.

The second Flo had explained, her mother's behavior made a lot of sense. I recall feeling protective of Flo, wanting to make things better for her and her mother, show them there were some decent guys left. But a couple days in, I began to feel like a fraud, because my heart wasn't in it the way it should be. I was doing the right thing for the sake of doing the right thing, not because I was head over heels for Flo.

And because of how disingenuous I myself was being, I probably hadn't noticed how fake Flo's comfort level with me was, either. Now I could see through some of her gives. She overcompensated with thoughtfulness when our relationship felt lacking. Again, these efforts made me feel guilty, and I tried to step up, rather than wonder why she was taking all the burden and blame on herself.

In fact, I kept comparing this parental visit to the times with Maggie's dad and stepmother in Texas. That had been idyllic, every second of it. All the natural chemistry reacting as if by design. And the more I tried to make things right in Townsville over that spring holiday, the more things felt wrong. Was this how Flo had always felt? And if so, why was she still with me?

At seven a.m. on the dot, I dropped Flo off at the airport, on fire with what the idea of Maggie and me having the city to ourselves would look like. Pretty fucking hot if that photo of her in her teddy meant anything.

OH, it was fun to watch Maggie squirm. The sick mother idea was a stroke of genius. You certainly can't argue with that.

I'd come up with the idea when we were at the conference. The second I saw Maggie come down the hallway to the fancy party, I'd escaped through the kitchen entrance and went up to Reg in his room.

He was feeling quite down. I knew what it was to be lonely, especially away from any friends or family, and so when I offered a bottle of wine and two glasses, he smiled and invited me in. Within seconds, he told me about how Maggie had attempted to seduce him and he'd pretended to be asleep.

"What's wrong with me?" he asked. He looked so innocent and hurt. I felt for him.

"Nothing. There's nothing wrong with you." I walked over to the minibar and popped a beer for him. "Here."

"Thanks." He took a long sip, staring out over the sea. "You know, Flo. Is she going to break up with me? Because even though she was trying to seduce me, it just seemed like she was going through the motions."

"You want the truth?"

His eyes scrunched. "Yeah, I think so."

"Yes, I think she's going to break up with you."

I walked over to the bed and put my arm around his shoulder. I wish there had been someone to do that for me. He closed his eyes and tears began to stream down his face.

"I know we don't belong together, but I'm scared, you know, Flo? Scared that I'll never be completely in love with anyone."

"I know exactly what you mean."

When I kissed him, he must have been hoping that maybe this would be it, because he kissed me with the most passion anyone has ever pressed into my lips.

TWENTY-SEVEN

MAGGIE

SHE SLEPT ON THE SOFA. George hadn't broken anything on Reg's face, but he'd given him a huge gash under his eye, and a nice lump on top of that, which made his eyelid so puffed and bruised his eyeball was completely concealed by it.

However, she only learned this from a letter in which Reg also said he was sleeping "elsewhere" tonight.

Dear Maggie,

Why was George so fucking mad at me, huh? What does he care? Because you're fucking him, aren't you? Is this why you wanted to break up with me? Well you know what? I am cheating on you! That's right! You're not the only one with secrets. And that's where I'm sleeping tonight. With someone who appreciates me. So I guess I win. Leaving it in a Dear John letter gives me a few extra points too.

What the fuck? She slept on the sofa because she couldn't bear to sleep in the bed she'd shared with Reg. In fact, she wanted to burn it. She knew he'd only written it in the letter rather than face her because he didn't want her to see what George had done to him. It would derail the bravado he was desperately trying to portray. Surprisingly, she slept better than she had in weeks. She dreamed about "accidentally" smashing into Reg's hurt cheekbone.

And then she woke in the morning and decided he wasn't worth another thought. She felt great, so she called into work, claimed food poisoning, showered and perfumed and wore that teddy from the sext she'd sent so that George could see it in person. She understood about fantasy, anticipation.

Today had been a long time in the making, and with the pent-up sexual spark pulsing through her and the energy she felt pulsing through George last night, this felt like diving into an ocean, boundless and unfathomable, stormy and most terrifying of all, completely beyond her control.

With Reg's confession and the very questionable behavior on Flo's part, Maggie had woken with much less resistance to giving into her desires. Last night had been a turning point. She was ready to feel George inside her.

She was hit with the physical memory of desire and terror existing side by side. Was it the terror that heightened her love so? If it was, there was something slightly fucked up about that. But weren't we all just massive psychological soups, just waiting to boil over, burn out, or simply cook down to nothing at all?

She'd lived with the everything of George and she'd lived without. Now she was going to block out that terrified part of her that understood it was vulnerability she was so haunted by. And she was going to pull up her big girl pants and give into every desire pulsing through her.

George came up to her place even though it was notoriously impossible to park on her street. He was exactly on time. She was in a black dress just sheer enough to let him see what was underneath. When he buzzed, she pressed to open the downstairs door, then cracked her unit's door and arranged herself on the kitchen counter, one bare leg dangling and the other curled around a fresh plate of bacon. Oops, her panties were showing.

When she heard the door creak, she picked up a piece, cooked exactly the way George liked it, stretchy with just the right crispness around the edges, hot bubbles of oil still flecked on its surface, and lowered the end of one strip between her open lips, tongue slipped out to taste.

George took one look and stopped dead in his tracks. Oh, it was clear he wanted her. And that sent a jolt to where she could already tell she was slick. Maggie took a fierce bite, closed her eyes in ecstasy as she chewed the salty perfection. "Mmmmm," she said, and licked her lips. His eyes were glued to her mouth.

She froze suddenly, mid-chew as if she'd just been struck by a thought and held out the other half.

"Hungry?" she said. There was a flicker of movement in his jeans.

"You have no idea." He walked toward her, slowly, the planes of his chiseled chest visible through his shirt. She ached to touch him.

She held the bacon strip out to him, the shape of her bite mark and her saliva at the end, and he took it in his mouth, swallowed it down, and sucked her outstretched fingers. Maggie gasped. She was pure desire. Within seconds, he was at her mouth, greedy, kissing, sucking, probing. He pushed the plate aside and pulled her to the edge of the counter so she was right up against him.

"Fuck me," she ordered. She forgot how she got with him, how uninhibited she was. She would never say those things to anyone else. But she didn't want tender. She didn't want love making. She wanted, needed, to satisfy this hunger, to become one with him.

He moaned into her mouth. What she hadn't forgotten, what she'd jammed her fingers inside herself thinking about too many times to count was the effect her dirty words had on him. Such an unshakable, brave man. And she could get him grunting, desperate, rock solid. For her. Her smile stretched her whole face. She could even feel her eyes change shape.

George reached for his belt. He unbuckled painfully slowly. Then he undid his button fly in one quick pull. And there it was. Encased in taut black boxer briefs. Exactly as remembered. The sight of it made her reach out.

His eyes went to the ceiling. The effect she was having on him propelled her. She was beneath the waist band. He was pulling at his jeans to get her there that much faster. In seconds the glorious length of him was freed and she was curling her hand around the width of him, pulling, and squirming her liquid core closer to him.

He reached up to yank his shirt up over his head and there he was, all hers. It was too much. They were both at each other. His fingers tickled at the edge of the tiny lacy strip separating her from him, then he pulled it aside, and his fingers were on her and in her, and their mouths were gnashing and neither of them could take it anymore. And they were squirming toward the illicit joining, the way they needed to feel each other.

The tip of him met her clit. Everything slowed. He slid around in the wet, edging closer to penetration as they both breathed and moaned like animals. And then, suddenly, his tip was at her opening. They looked at each other in the junkie-about-to-have-a-high way they always had, and then with a thrust, he was in. George. Was. Inside. Her. Her lids fluttered. Shivers shook every inch of her.

Maggie's hands clutched at his arms, his tangled in her hair. There was nothing in the world but them, there, now, in a narcotic haze of feel and touch, sensation.

"I'm going to come," she said when she felt the sensations build to a breaking point.

"Come," he said, his hands now at her waist, thrusting more quickly, losing himself to it. She yelled out as she let go, the release a rush, her body aquiver. And then he was gone, collapsing in that incredible moan in the shape of her name. "Maggie," he whispered, tugging her even tighter around him, her pulsing picking up again.

As they clutched each other in the aftermath, she glimpsed in the periphery that addict high quell too quickly, giving way to the covetous nature of feeling he was *hers*, the desperation for it all to happen again. This kind of thing was not meant to last. It was what she'd always jokingly said after sex. Because it was always that intense between them.

She wouldn't dare say it now. But was it hanging there, unsaid between them anyway. No. She pushed it away. That was fear talking. She knew George. She knew this was love. And that was that.

There were big plans to go to Coogee, to their old spot, but there was a shower, and when she saw him grow erect at soaping up her clit, they were at it again. This time, he knelt and flicked his tongue around where he'd just washed her, delicately, the way that drove her nuts, then harder and faster until she came in his mouth.

"You want more, don't you?" he said. He was a man possessed.

She nodded, turned around, lifted her ass and leaned her arms against the tiles, craned her neck to watch.

"Give it to me," she said.

When he entered her this time it was harder, rougher, but it couldn't be deep enough, hard enough for her. He made her feel like a woman. He made her feel like they'd discovered the meaning of life.

Was it ratcheted up a few thousand notches because it still felt slightly wrong, not the above-board trajectory they'd originally planned, but instead a secret thing between the two of them? She hoped not, but she didn't let her mind dwell too deeply there.

He pumped her expertly, until again she built and built to climax. This time she screamed out. And once again, in the catching of her breath, she glimpsed a view of herself, thinking those things that she couldn't believe she'd thought. Getting turned on by the idea of fucking Flo's boyfriend.

It was ugly in this light and scared her, though she knew it was just a random string in a massive tangle that couldn't be categorized all good or all bad. She hated to be unsure of herself, and this in turn made her clutch him tighter. Because the ugly scariness seemed to be pointing to the obvious unreality of it all. This was not a thing that could last. There it was again.

She kissed him harder and went down on her knees and took him in her mouth and brought him deeper and deeper inside her throat, until she couldn't see that ugliness anymore. All there was in the whole world that she could see was them.

TWENTY-EIGHT

GEORGE

WE DIDN'T LEAVE that unit for two whole days and nights. All that existed was a fug of sex and bacon and delivery pizza and endless baths in which we spoke about all the things we'd missed in each other's lives in the past four years, and then we clung to each other until we had to mark our mutual territory again.

It felt incredible. I forgot how much *fun* we had together. In between the sex and the serious conversation there was this incredible banter, this mutual vision of the world—enriched with two incredibly different journeys through life—that made everything make sense. This clear path to our future, it was back. And I had to remind myself that this was how I'd gotten in trouble in the first place. I'd taken it for granted. But I wasn't going to do that again.

"Maggie," I said on the morning we both had to go back to work, "I love you more than anything in this world. I am not going on this deployment. I shouldn't have done that the first time. I own that. You and me. That is all that matters in this world. We've got enough money from my pension and whatever else I'll do workwise here and there to be happy for the rest of our lives. I'm leaving the army. I choose you."

She was quiet, but I could tell from the way she followed my eyes that she saw deep down to the truth of what I was saying. She knew how much I loved her. I felt a great relief. I had wanted to make this right for so long.

That was a lot of reality. It had taken me so long to say those words the right way, so that she understood, that I didn't expect her to know what to do with them. Instead, I spoke the language we had always been expert at. I took her in my arms, pressed every inch of my body against every inch of her body and kissed her as fiercely as I felt.

Within seconds it was a frenzied mashing of mouths and my cock pulsed to be inside her. We ground against each other in ecstasy, my tip so close, Maggie's delicious gasping for me to be inside.

It was the most natural thing in the world to say it now. "I love you." The only thing that made me happier than uttering that was hearing them come out of her mouth at exactly the same time. See? Perfection.

TWENTY-NINE

MAGGIE

SHE HAD to go to work. Her boss had literally said, "If you don't come in for this investor meeting today you will no longer have a job."

It was a good thing she had claimed food poisoning rather than a cold or the flu. She would have been looking pretty shady about now. Because she was glowing. Literally glowing. Even before she put makeup on. Fuck. She felt like a million bucks. A billion bucks. She knew all the stereotypes about love and how cheesy it looked to everyone else who was just jealous, but they *should* be jealous. This was the most incredible feeling ever.

No wonder she'd been so blah for the past few years she hadn't even been able to bring herself to break up with Reg. Because life was literally *nothing* compared to this. And every day without George had felt exactly like that. What did it matter who she slept next to, who mechanically brought her to orgasm from the right combination of manipulation? That was not sex. That was survival.

In the cloud of fucking brilliance that was now her life, she nearly forgot about Flo altogether. If it wasn't exactly an erasure of memory; it was a tidal wave of incredible feels that swept away the Flo complication in its force in a way that said *every-thing* is better this way. It's all great. It will work out.

But now she was going back to work and Flo wasn't there. She could see holes in her logic.

To make matters worse, Flo rang right in the middle of the investor meeting. Her phone was on silent and she watched it ring out with dread in her heart. Then the missed call notif-ication dinged. Flo. Flo. Flo. She was all over her phone, reminding her she'd just spent the last two days fucking her boyfriend. No tidal wave was going to make that look good.

Still. Flo had been doing some crazy shit, which didn't excuse her sleeping with George behind her back, but which certainly put a complicated lens over the whole thing. Flo had blocked their phones, lied—a lot. Why? She knew. Obviously. But then what was she playing at?

The standard brain pathway from here was bunny boiling. But that was in films. This was real life.

FLO: CALL ME. SOS.

Maggie's heart plummeted. She swallowed. That would teach her to use food poisoning as an excuse. There was audible swirling in her stomach. Her hand went to her mouth. A few pairs of eyes, including that of the boss who'd threatened her job, darted her way, looking revolted.

"Excuse me," she said, grabbing for her phone, telling herself people always grabbed their phones when they left a room, even if they were going to throw up, maybe especially, so they could call for a lifeline if necessary. It didn't look guilty, she assured herself as she ran toward the toilets and tried to quell her guts to call Flo.

"Maggie!" Flo picked up immediately.

Was that an angry tone? Concerned? Grateful? Oh, what did she know? "What's going on, Flo?" It felt good just to ask. She needed to be out with it.

. . .

"WHAT DO YOU THINK, Maggie? Is he going to break up with me?" She asked the question as if she *knew* the explanation had something to do with Maggie. They weren't talking about Flo's mother. So did that mean they were all calling bullshit on that story now?

When Maggie didn't respond, she repeated the question. "Do you think he might break up with me?"

"George? I don't know, honey." Maggie spoke down into her own chest, standing with her head against the cool tile

"George? Who's George?"

Oh no. What had she done? Maggie sat up with a splash. "Sorry. I was confusing him with someone else."

"That seems odd. Especially since George is Lionel's middle name."

She knew. She totally knew. So why was she still playing this game? "You know me—odd!" Maggie tried to laugh it off, but she was dying to be out with it. The Freudian slip was exhibit A.

"Yeah, that's about right. You should check in on him for me."

"Me?" Maggie stared at herself over the bathroom sink.

"You know what?"

"Mmm-hmm?" Maggie stepped back, wrung her hands, tried to roll out her neck.

"Why don't you go to ANZAC Day with him? He's speaking and I bet he'd love to look out and see you there in the audience."

"Me?"

"Mmmm-hmmm."

"Okay, I guess." Oh, the unsaid. "I was planning to go anyway."

"Great," Flo said. "And when I get back you and I need to talk."

The day dragged on as Maggie obsessed over Flo's parting remarks. The whole thing was shady. Maggie raked through her history with Flo, trying to pick out bits that didn't add up. But Flo had always been such a perfect fit for Maggie. It was like she'd known her even before they met. It didn't make sense.

MAGGIE: *I think she knows. I called you george by mistake and then she said we need to talk when she gets back. Asked me to go to anzac day with you.*

GEORGE: *What is she? My babysitter?*

MAGGIE: *So you don't want me to go with you?*

GEORGE: *Of course I do. Please wear something low-cut.*

She smiled despite the stress of the situation.

MAGGIE: *Can't you stop thinking about sex for one minute?*

GEORGE: *Not with you.*

MAGGIE: *Why did you change your name anyway?*

GEORGE: *Couldn't stand hearing another woman say my name. It's meant to be said in your voice.*

MAGGIE: *Good answer.*

GEORGE: *Meet me early*

MAGGIE: *Wish I could. This investor thing is going all night and i haven't made a very good impression so far.*

GEORGE: *Maybe show them the picture of you in that lingerie?*

MAGGIE: *Going now.*

GEORGE: *Well, that's one of us. I'm going to have to sit here for a while until things cool down.*

MAGGIE: *You're very bad.*

GEORGE: *That's not helping.*

THIS WAS PERFECT. ANZAC Day was going to be the climax. I had an excellent show planned. Maggie had nearly spilled everything when she called Lionel *George* by mistake, but I shut that down. It was an excellent touch to let her stew in that for a while. The guilt about dishonoring our friendship was the biggest hurdle in their love affair, so it was apt that it would be the last problem to be overcome in their love story. Then straight onto the HEA.

But this was the climax. So it was going to be B. I. G.

When I saw Reg's eye and the nasty cut beneath it, I couldn't have been more pleased. The drama! This was going down as the world's most exciting coupling, and just think who was responsible for it!

My mind cut to images of the grateful couple with Reg and me having a double date at the Rocks, under the moonlight. It was incredible that we'd both find our happily ever afters together. See, I couldn't have planned everything.

I took my serendipitous new relationship with Reg as evidence that I was doing everything right, and the universe was congratulating me on a job well done. And the best part—I wouldn't be the victim.

I'd purposely left out any reference to my mum's hospitalization. We were transitioning into the next phase here, working up to the highest tension point, and it was just right to keep some unknowns mixed in there.

The big reveal would be the high point of the whole thing. That I'd seen Maggie in the photo, tracked her down out of jealousy, and then had grown to love her so much, seen how deeply they belonged with each other, and then brought them back together! Who doesn't love a redemption story? Especially with the added twist of me and Reg finding solace in each other.

Of course, Reg would be there for the big reveal, too, and I worried slightly that he would be angry with me for sabotaging his relationship. But then I felt sure it would be okay because now we'd found each other, and here again, was evidence of fate at work. I was working on pure feeling at this point. It was so strong, this growing sense of universal rightness that I had to believe I was headed in the right direction.

THIRTY-ONE

MAGGIE

MAGGIE ARRIVED EARLY to the dawn service. It was freezing. She was exhausted from the investor circus Five Dinners corporate had put on.

After the morning meeting, she'd made up for her strange exit by making nice with all three of the bigwigs at a Make It Yourself lunch in the Five Dinners test kitchen. One had a kid studying in Texas where her father lived and tried to impress her with his version of a southern drawl (she'd heard worse), another had said he'd been following her blog entries about using the new vegan ingredients and that was one of the main reasons they'd decided to invest.

They could see the way "the food climate was changing," he said, and Five Dinners Done! were at the helm. They had the right style, the right menu, and the right look and feel. There was money to be made, and they had the image to make it, according to him. And she was key to that image. The third one seemed to be enjoying her cleavage. And she was too tired to make a big deal about that. It was enough at the moment that things were swinging her way.

The meeting had then gone onto dinner and she'd

completely forgotten that Flo had booked the same Harbour restaurant at Circular Quay where she'd run into George on that incredible double date. It all came flashing back to her, the absolute shock, the torrent of emotions, the recognition. Right then and there, in that moment she'd spotted him across the table, she knew she was stupidly in love with George. Always had been.

A flush crept up her neck as she thought about the conversation she'd had with Flo earlier. She hadn't been surprised by the George revelation, had she? She'd just let it go with a comment about that being his middle name. There was something very strange going on, stranger even than Flo blocking their phones and coming up with a fake illness for her mother, and her stomach did a little somersault when she tried to think what it might be.

Stop. She told herself now wasn't the time. She couldn't afford another near-barfing episode when they were this close to sealing the deal with the investors. But when that same gorgeous glamazon from the George dinner led them on that labyrinthine walk to their table, she said to Maggie, "I remember you. You're that woman Flo was obsessed with. Watch out for that one."

"You know Flo?" The walk wasn't too long. She needed to get as much information as she could without drawing the attention of the investors. She spoke quietly and hoped the hostess would take the hint.

Thankfully the hostess spoke in a discreet tone as she continued. "She used to work here. Used to try to fix up customers. She'd pretend one had bought a drink for the other, they'd get to talking and she'd moon over the whole thing, talk about how good her eye was for matchmaking."

"Matchmaking?"

"Yeah. She did have a decent eye for it. Always reading romance novels, her head in the clouds. Quite a few nasty hookups on her account, if you know what I mean." She winked. "Oh, the best was, though, this one night a guy she'd pulled this on was approached by the woman he supposedly bought a drink for, then his wife walked in and got the wrong idea. Got real messy up in here."

"How'd you know she was obsessed with me?"

"She has a photo of you and her boyfriend. I told her it was totally weird. But she said there was something in that photo, that you two were meant to be together."

"When was this?"

She blew out a huge sigh that didn't quite go with her spotless look. It made her real. "Must've been about eighteen months ago."

Right when she interviewed with Maggie at Five Dinners!

They'd arrived at the table, right next to the one where they'd sat last time. "Thanks," she said, realizing her hands were trembling. So many lies. Another case of putting her trust in the wrong person. What the fuck was wrong with her? Was she missing the part of her brain that filtered out toxic people? What about George? Could she trust her feelings about him?

"Hey, don't say anything to Flo about it. I probably shouldn't have said anything. She didn't seem all that stable. I'd hate to think I caused her more stress."

Maggie nodded. The woman handed out the oversize menus ceremoniously, placed each person's napkin on their lap, then came back around to Maggie. "Hey, one more thing. Did you wind up with him?"

"Not sure yet."

The woman nodded, sagely, as if Maggie had finally gotten something right.

· · ·

IN THIS PART OF AUSTRALIA, ANZAC Day was considered the beginning of winter. When you were allowed to start turning your heater on. As for the event itself, popular culture dictated that it was a comparatively measly sacrifice to wake up before dawn in the freezing to commemorate those who'd given their lives for us.

Maggie tried not to fashion her thoughts of the battle of Gallipoli from the Mel Gibson film, but she had watched it more than once with George and she couldn't help but picture some of the scenes as she took a seat in the fourth row behind the VIP seats taped with computer printed names of generals and ministers. At least it was a break from doubting her instincts about who to trust.

Maggie looked down at the program to see when George was speaking. This reminded her of the many speeches where she'd sat and looked up at him, amazed and proud, and a million other feelings she couldn't—and wouldn't dare to—pin down. She was wearing her medal slide, which only had three medals: The Army Commendation Medal, Non-Commissioned Officer Professional Development Ribbon, and The Army Achievement Medal, both of which she was very proud.

Even before her medal-earning days, she'd sacrificed for service. It could be said that her entire wellbeing had been sacrificed for military life. But that was nothing compared to eighteen-year-old boys getting their faces blown off. She knew that. Which was why she'd never given any actual credence to her "issues," and she knew from where she sat at this moment that this was precisely why she'd wound up where she had, instead of married with two kids by now to the man she loved. If she was alive and intact, she should be happy, not worrying over first world problems like building the right relationships. Fabulous was *having* a life.

But now she wasn't so sure. Everything had gradients of

color that she hadn't allowed herself to indulge in before—probably, if she was being honest with herself, for fear of coming up short. There was living. And then there was that thing she'd been doing with George for forty-eight hours. Fuck, there was no comparison. She wanted the George thing. But what if she was wrong about him the way she had been about Flo?

"I'm *right*" was the phrase here. Couldn't even get the full "all right" out. Too dramatic for these stoics. But farther down the road, she saw the hole in that logic. If we didn't address our issues, they were going to come and bite us in the ass. Enter Flo. She was one hell of an ass biter.

Only Maggie didn't know if the wakeup call was to show her she *should* be with George, or that she'd better realize she didn't know a thing about people. And that she should quit at 'right' and forget the fantasy of the George Thing once and for all.

She closed her eyes and tried to remind herself what she was doing here—remembering the sacrifice of the fallen. A couple of inhales and exhales, and Maggie opened her eyes to see George waiting to take the podium. His gaze was trained right on her. He smiled when their eyes met, and he mouthed, "I love you." Her body turned to liquid. One tick for the George Thing.

A couple of people sitting ahead of her turned to see who he'd been speaking to. There was some smiling, whispering, and pointing.

George spoke of one soldier's specific account of the events of that fateful day, surviving on "two biscuits and water" for twenty-four hours while his friends were shot to death and the lucky ones suffered sniper wounds around him, rough crosses being carved to mark graves, hand grenades rendering the dead unrecognizable but for their dog tags. She tried not to pay heed to the tears streaming down her face.

Maggie found herself overcome when she tried to picture the young Lieutenant (pronounced *lef-tenant* over here) drinking tea, the screaming and shrapnel all around him, as he tried to keep his mind from the horrors for a minute of normalcy, recalling how that day he was lucky enough after his tea to change his socks.

George was an incredible speaker and wasn't happy with the status quo: *thank you for coming; this is why we're here; thank you; enjoy your day*. He cared too deeply about the topic he was honoring and wanted the audience to understand and see things in an enlightened, personal way, not just the lazy way we'd come to know. He was passionate about this kind of education to a fault.

She'd often wondered whether people would ever achieve the level of understanding he desired for them. She remembered how he'd often get frustrated by people's comfort in their ignorance. It never bothered her in quite the same way. Most people lived in small bubbles. She forgave people their survival methods. Lord knows hers weren't anything award winning. But she respected George's M.O. and she often felt like a better citizen of the world with him.

Could this goal of perfection have something to do with why he hadn't stopped her from leaving him before Afghanistan? The more he spoke, articulating the most complex ideas clearly, irrefutably, the more she felt generous toward his motives and open to how their different world views may have clashed back then. This made sense. That's really what it had all been about.

He was a good man. The best. If it was his job to go, he had to go. He'd only been in his twenties, after all. He'd said as much himself the other night. If there was anything the two of them had fucked up in the past, it was honesty, generosity in affording the benefit of the doubt.

Instead, they'd hedged their bets and protected their egos. She made a decision then and there to trust her feelings toward him—regardless of how off base she'd been about Flo. There was a clear future path she could see before her. And it led to the George Thing. And George's *thing*, lots of George's thing.

Shake it off, she told herself as George continued to captivate the audience. She looked at him on the elevated stage and felt her heart soar. This was love. No matter what happened with Flo, she was certain of what she had with George.

As if he read her mind, he looked right at her.

He was speaking to her. As if no one else mattered. Even in the face of all this horror, or maybe even because of it, he'd never change his view of that, his expression said.

There were two speakers after George, and the last one recited the words that always got her:

They shall grow not old;
As we that are left grow old;
Age shall not weary them,
Nor the years condemn.
At the going down of the sun and in the morning
We will remember them.

THEN A HAUNTING BUGLE rendition of *Reveille* heralded in the most poignant moment of silence she'd ever had. She and George held their gaze the whole time, a silent exchange of everything she thought and felt. She was certain of it.

As George descended the podium and everyone made a beeline across the parade ground, past the two-hundred-year-old sandstone offices for the complimentary breakfast—she watched an ancient woman in a delicate pillbox hat lay a wreath at the foot of the memorial where a placard was inscribed with the words: "Live life - Dream Big - Take Risks. It honors their sacrifice."

George came and squeezed her hand, kissed her like he meant it, right there in front of everyone on this most poignant of days. She swooned. Everything was as it was meant to be.

LATER THAT EVENING, Maggie sighed as they walked under the heating vents at the Paddington Returned Service League. She'd never get used to the opposite season cycle. Friends of hers in New York were just taking their coats off and showing leg while she was gearing up for a whole lotta cold. But this year she was going to stay warm. George's arm around her assured her of that.

Because of the 100th anniversary of Gallipoli, the army had gone all out. Tons of camouflage netting was suspended from the ceiling, fairy lights twisted up in it, old bits of barbed wire, and all the servers in military kit from World War I.

Everywhere the eye could see, time had rewound. It was as if they weren't in the present at all, and on some level, that was liberating. Outside, the harbour was like a beacon of success. They'd made it, the spectacular lights of the bridge, the opera house and the Quay in the distance seem to have said. They fucking did it. And beauty—and their love—could thrive again.

Looking back at George, she said, "Remember that exhibit we went to when I first came here—in Canberra at the National Museum? It focused on the year 1913 before the war, how hopeful everything was, how everyone thought their happiness was untouchable?"

He nodded, grabbed for her hand. "We were a bit like that too, weren't we?" He kissed her.

His lips were wonderful but talk of the exhibit took Maggie

immediately back to her first days here, George educating her on her new home in his lovely, passionate way. It had been hard, living amongst these things with the ghost of him hanging everywhere.

She had a thought and pulled back from the kiss. Instead of keeping that thought to herself, she shared it with him.

"I'm sorry," he replied, squeezing her hand to show he meant it. "I am going to spend the rest of my life making that up to you. You are not to be taken for granted."

Now it was her turn to nod. And then she leaned in for the fiercest kiss they'd shared yet. Look at them, already getting smug in their happiness. Wasn't it wonderful?

"We're table number ten." He handed her a card.

Maggie could feel her face heat as his fingers brushed hers. He led her by the hand to the table, despite the curious onlookers who knew Flo, and that Maggie hadn't been in the picture for some time.

AS I MADE my way to the bar, it was a complete existence. Maggie waiting for me a few metres away, looking like that because of what we'd been doing in her bed, on her floor, and in her kitchen, skin to skin all day after the speech and breakfast.

"I like watching you," Maggie said, as soon as I came to our table with two pints. We probably didn't need anything else to drink, but what was ANZAC Day for a veteran without going to the Returned Services League? The RSL is like Mecca to soldiers on a day like this.

She looked incredible. Maggie was in uniform and she could rock it. I told her so.

"Thank you," she said. It was quite a feeling to know your opinion made a woman stand taller—not because she needed to be validated, no Maggie was too strong for that, but because you meant so much to her.

She moved her gloves aside to make way for the beers. God, she was so prepared! Who remembered gloves this early in the season? You were meant to freeze, then think about bringing them, forget them a couple more times, and *then* ball them up in your coat pocket for the winter.

These things used to drive me crazy about her. But now I tugged at the string of each such memory and found them connected to a big old ball of tenderness and yearning that tangled up with the idea of what we were doing this afternoon in her bed, and I found myself needing to clear my throat.

"I am so happy, right now," I said to her. *Tell her everything.* It didn't come naturally to me. But when I saw the look on her face, when she'd said that thing to me about living with the ghost of me everywhere, I knew just what she meant and how much she'd suffered. I understood why it was important to be open with her.

She stood from her barstool and brushed her body against mine, and whispered in my ear, "me too," then tugged on my earlobe with her teeth. Yes, I could get used to this speaking your mind thing.

THIRTY-THREE
GEORGE

TOWARD ELEVEN P.M., it was getting rowdy up in the RSL. Maggie felt amazing, sitting on my lap, my arms wrapped tightly around her, my face in that perfect spot on her neck. It was a strange, new, wonderful sensation. For the first time in a long time, I could see the future stretching out before me. *Our* future.

But there was still something that needed to be addressed, and Maggie must have been chewing on it, despite—or perhaps because of—the perfection of the last seventy-two hours. "Promise me we'll talk to Flo when she gets back," she said. I still couldn't believe all the shit that hostess had told Maggie. I felt like talking to Flo like I wanted to have a few root canals. But I knew Maggie needed the closure—whatever that looked like.

"That's some kind of dirty talk," I said. She smiled into the side of my cheek, I felt her lips curl. Me. I did that. Finally.

"We will. We'll talk to Flo right away." I held her tightly and let my lips linger on that edge of her smile. I felt her whole body purr with her delicious pleasure sound.

"What are you going to talk to me about?" We both swiveled suddenly at the sound of Flo's voice.

"Flo!" Maggie stood, smoothed down the front of her skirt. There was no covering up the fact that she had been sitting on my lap, making sex kitten sounds, but God love her for trying.

"I thought I might find you both here," she said.

Did she? What a freak. Is that why she'd told Maggie to accompany me today? For some kind of stand off?

"You're back early!" Maggie said.

"Yup, Mum did great. They discharged her."

"Didn't you say they keep you for two days after a carotid artery?" Maggie asked. Bless her for trying to find sense in Flo's actions.

But wait. *A carotid artery?* Flo said her mother was in for a cardiac procedure. I looked to her, dubious, and she wore that irritating mask she put on from time to time, which made her look like a robot more than a person, as if none of the rules applied to her because she was in a relationship with someone who didn't love her properly. How many times had I fallen into that trap? Well, those days were over.

"Flo?" I said. "I see what you've done there. Two different stories—a chance for us to work out the inconsistency. You got us!" Best to appease crazy people. Maybe if she got what she wanted she'd go away. At least Maggie didn't have to feel guilty anymore. Who am I kidding? She's so nice, she's going to feel guilty anyway.

Flo's smile spread even further. She slowly clapped, flicking her gaze between Maggie and me. She wanted to be the hero. As long as I made it very fucking clear to her that she would never meddle again, I guess I could give her this moment. Because in the end, we were together. And she had made it happen.

Still, she looked terrifyingly ecstatic, as if she had just lit a fire and was now front and center to watch it blaze everything.

Now Maggie shrugged. Even amidst this—which was about to become the winning origin story of any *how did you get together* competition—our connection was solid. She was beautiful, smart, she got me, and I fucking loved her, no matter how we'd reunited.

There was a strange look on Flo's face which didn't match her words. She changed the topic, as if to say she was pulling the strings, one thing at a time, on my schedule. I wanted to wipe that smug look off her face.

"How was George's speech?" she said. "He takes these speaking invitations very seriously. Haven't been in bed before me in about two weeks, have you? Up burning the midnight oil to prepare."

Her tone was off. There was something more than the you-don't-love-me righteousness in it, and I could tell Maggie had caught it too. Her manic smile only made things worse.

"His speech was incredible. It really touched me," Maggie said, trying to speak slowly, set a pace.

"I'll bet."

THIRTY-FOUR

MAGGIE

AFTER HER COMMENT insinuating intimacy between George and Maggie, Flo appeared to have opened some mental floodgates.

The reunited couple, so happy moments ago exchanged a look: *this is it*. Guilt could've been shading their interpretation, but Maggie didn't think so. Flo *had* lied about her mother's hospitalization; she *did* know about Maggie and George, and now she was making some kind of show of her reveal. And definitely enjoying it.

"All right, Flo. So what's next?" George asked. People were beginning to turn and look, even amidst the noise and applause of the Two-Up game *still* going in the far corner.

Flo shook her head. She was playing star of the show. It didn't suit her. "Oh, look at you two!"

"Flo, what's going on?" Maggie said, trying to stay calm.

"Ooooh, this is going to be so much fun! The climax is the best part. You know, where everything seems impossible. Very dramatic. You two have overcome so many obstacles, care of *moi*. And now, just when everything's going so well, it all comes smashing down in pieces."

Maggie's heart raced.

"Been looking for this?" Flo said and fished around in her coat pocket, pulling out a print of the same photo Maggie used for a bookmark in her Gallipoli book and on her phone for George's contact details—the two of them on the Manly Ferry. It must have been the copy she'd given to George. Flo dangled it between two fingers in front of George's face.

His jaw tightened. His blue eyes were ice. He snatched the photo from her.

Her face fell, like she'd been expecting an entirely different reaction.

"Where did you get that?" he asked.

"I found it in the bottom of your sock drawer where you kept taking peeks at it when you thought I wasn't paying attention."

Maggie and George caught each other's eye. He gave a small shrug and her heart went out to him. *Of course,* his gesture said.

He slowly tucked the print in the pocket over his chest. He patted it, looked at Maggie as if to point out where she belonged —in his heart.

Oh, how she loved him in that moment. The air between them positively vibrated with their connection.

Then he turned to Flo, fury reigniting his features. "You saw Maggie in that photo and then you hunted her down. Is that why you decided suddenly to become a chef? Interviewed at her company? Holy shit. This is psychotic, Flo."

She clearly didn't like his word choice. Flo's features hardened, her eyes squeezed in anger. She cried and screamed and called him bad names, but then she stopped suddenly, cleared her throat and held out her fingers to frame George and Maggie in an imaginary photo and smiled. This seemed to calm her.

"You two belong together. It was so obvious from that photo. You never looked at me like that, George. I made it my mission to get you two back together. Guess who proposed partners go to the conference? That's right! Me! Guess who put laxative in c's coffee so I had to take over her duties for you guys to talk. Me again! Mobile phone blocking? Yup, you guessed it. Good old Flo."

It was silent, deadly silent. Obviously not the reaction she'd expected because her features rearranged themselves once again from excitement to fury. Flo swallowed again, drew a steadying breath.

"Tell me this," Flo said, "you aren't the steady, straight-up guy you are with me, are you? You are passionate and fiery and wild and all the things you throw into your work, when you're with Maggie, aren't you?"

George opened his mouth.

"No. You don't have to tell me. I know. I know everything. You're a heartbreaker, George. You're the kind of man that ruins a girl for life. And that's even when you only give a fraction of yourself. I can't imagine what you did to Maggie all those years ago. She got all of you. I know she did. And why shouldn't she? She's, well, she's Maggie. You never stood a chance. And yet, you still mucked it up. But now I've shown you the light, haven't I?"

She was working herself up. That was clear.

Then she took Maggie's champagne and sipped long and loud. "I do know this is the way it's meant to be. You should know that. But that doesn't mean it hurts any less. Deep down, I wish it could have been me that you felt that way for."

"Flo—"

She showed me a stiff palm. "Don't. Even you can't explain this one away."

"I wouldn't dare attempt it. But I want you to know you deserve love like this. Everyone does. I can see how your jealousy got the best of you, and frankly, it's disturbing. And I do want to pummel you right now for the pain you caused Maggie, for the deception. For the way she nearly gave her happiness up for you! God, Flo, you can't play with people that way."

"Like the way you played with me? Keeping me around even though you loved someone else?"

"You're right. Who can say which is worse? I just handled it less insanely. But the 'normal' way still amounted to wasting your time, making you doubt yourself, causing you pain, playing with your life, I guess. For that, I'm sorry. And it sounds like you had good intentions for Maggie and me, though you manipulated us terribly. Now, I'm going to have to insist that you stay out of our lives."

But Flo wasn't ready to give up just yet. "Maggie, look at me. I can see what this is doing to you. Now you're saying, I thought I knew Flo. Just like I thought I knew George all those years ago. And you're thinking this proves you're wrong again about George."

"You're right, Flo. You do know me well. But your deception doesn't cancel out what's between George and me. I may have been wrong about you, but I know I'm right about George." She grabbed for George's hands and squeezed. She meant every word. That was obvious.

"I bet you want to kiss her right now, don't you?" Flo said. "It's the perfect moment."

He looked to Maggie, a corner of his mouth perking up. Could it all really work out so well?

"But not so fast!" Flo trilled. "I've got one other trick up my sleeve. "Maggie's got a little secret she never told you, and I don't think it'd be quite right to have all this out in the open and just let that one go. It's a pretty big one."

No. She wouldn't tell her about the time she'd nearly cheated on George!

Flo was nearly bursting with glee.

George turned to Maggie and she knew she had to be out with it before Flo. It was the only way to show a little courage, though she knew as soon as the words were out, she would walk away, away from all of this. Every word Flo had uttered about her worries was right, and even though she'd faced those fears, decided to take a chance anyway, here was yet another landmine in their path. This ugly revelation was the nail in the coffin. She'd felt all along this was too good to be true. Just like it always did, the other shoe had to drop at some point. Why had she tried to convince herself things could be any different? This time at least she'd end it honestly. Now.

"I nearly cheated on you before we broke up, before your deployment." She forced herself to look in his eyes as she confessed. And she could sense every nuance of his shock and pain at the words.

Flo looked cheated. Still, she was clearly desperate to hear George's response.

"What? Why didn't you tell me?"

"I know there's no excuse. You and I hadn't been honest about our needs and things fell apart because of it. We dealt with them in all the wrong ways. I was trying to jolt myself into leaving you, because I didn't want to, but I also felt so deserted by you when you were deploying. And this time, we put it all out there—nearly—and it seemed like we could make it right.

"But it's obvious there's too much harm done. What I did was unforgiveable. Let myself go back to another man's apartment with the intent of sleeping with him. I hate to think of it. What a coward I was! Anything to protect myself from the pain of your leaving. I should have told you as soon as we started to reunite. But I know how you are about honesty and honor. So even though it was festering, I was ashamed. And now it's too late. I'm sorry, George. We missed our chance. Look at this! It's so fucked up! The world is trying desperately to keep us apart. I think it's time we listened." She held his gaze as long as she could stand, so he'd know how hard this was for her.

"Please don't come after me," she pleaded with him.

Maggie made it to the entrance. And then there was the inside of a taxi, with a musty smell. Then the warmth of the night, and the stars George had walked her through all those years ago, and the damned stringy bark trees he'd made sound so incredibly beautiful that she never walked past one without thinking about him.

And then her front door. The stairs to her flat. The creak. Reg's bike hung on pegs. But inside, no Reg. Just Maggie, her same old problems coming home to roost. Alone. The way she always wound up because she had no clue what made people tick, really. And she tried not to think how she'd been so close, how she'd been *there* with George. Because this time, she didn't know how she'd come back from the pain.

THIRTY-FIVE
GEORGE

I SLEPT off the ANZAC Day hangover and woke, gray and starving for bacon, and sick to death of Flo and everything to do with Flo. But that was weakness. I wasn't with Maggie because I'd fucked it up all those years ago, not because of Flo, psycho hose-beast that she was.

Did the idea of Maggie in the arms of another man make me sick to my stomach? You bet your ass. But was it her fault? Abs-o-fucking-lutely not. I own that. I threw her into that guy's arms. And I would never make that mistake again. And she'd stopped before anything happened. That meant something, and I knew it. Because she'd clearly wanted to show herself she was done with me. And she hadn't been able to go through with it.

Now I stared at that photo of me and Maggie on the ferry ride to Manly after I picked her up from Sydney airport all those years ago when she emigrated to start our lives. Our faces were pressed together, and we were stupidly, unthinkingly happy. Still tanned from the American summer, all those barbe-cues, the tiny swimsuits she wore.

Our lives were about to begin. We'd said it, jokingly, on the phone in the days while I awaited her arrival, while I lovingly chose furnishings and bed linens for my Maggie, possessed by something I'd never experienced prior. *I'm coming across the world to you,* she'd said. *We're about to start our lives,* I said. I'd never spoken like that before. Or after. How could I have let that sputter out and die? I deserved this. I was so ridiculously stupid.

I needed to up my game if I was going to make this right once and for all. If I didn't act fast, and hugely, Maggie would never trust me—she'd never trust anyone—again. Not only had I fucked things between us, again, but I'd also played a key role in ruining the best friendship she claims she ever had. I forgave her for the near-cheat, but would she forgive me?

This was not a time for text messaging, for worthless apologies. I knew exactly what I was going to do, and how I was going to do it.

THIRTY-SIX

MAGGIE

MAGGIE WOKE up with a sandpaper tongue and a headache across her eyes. Reg was burning toast in the kitchen, she thought. But no, that wasn't right. Then her mind sent a lure back through last night. *Oh fuck. Oh, last night.*

She put the blanket back over her head. But then threw it right back. The time for inaction was over. She didn't know what her next move was, but it wasn't going to be nothing. And it wasn't going to be waiting around for whatever life—or someone interfering in her life—threw at her.

But first, she heard Reg say, "Oh shit! Burnt again."

She steadied herself and took a long sip of water, raked her hair back into a ponytail and made her way into the kitchen. "Watcha doin' here, Reg? We broke up, remember?"

"Have a look at my eye and ask me if I remember."

It was yellowing, which meant it was healing. Maggie chose to take this as a sign. They'd all get there.

"I'm sorry about that, Reg. Really."

Reg must have felt that sympathy was inadequate. He raised his voice. "You don't need me anymore! I was a Band-Aid—from what?—I don't know, because you are unknowable."

A nod was all she'd give him. Emotionless, the way you're meant to scold a child. She was surprised how good at it she was.

"You really hurt me, Maggie. I feel used."

"You're right. For that, I'm also sorry."

"For *that?*"

"Well, you weren't exactly generous to me, Reg."

Reg rubbed the back of his head, his lids fluttered. "And you didn't encourage much generosity, Maggie."

"I know."

His eyes shot open. "There's something wrong with you."

"I know. But I'm working on it."

He got right in her face. "I do have one tidbit you don't know."

She could feel his spit above her lip. "Oh yeah, what's that?"

"Flo and I are together now."

Okay. Now that, she hadn't been expecting.

THE LAST PLACE Maggie wanted to go was work, but now that the investors were officially signed on, Maggie's responsibilities had grown. She played a key role in keeping them happy and abreast of what the company was doing. She needed to keep her eye on the ball.

Unfortunately, the ball was shaky. Everything was shaky. Her hangover was epic. A greasy egg sandwich was meant to put some life back into her but only made her feel more nauseated.

Apparently, Flo had given her notice the previous night, and by the time Maggie got to work, it was as if she had never worked there. Her desk was bare and there was a temp in her chair. A young guy with long shaggy hair held back at the top with a rubber band.

She called George to see if he would forgive her, despite how adamant she'd been last night because this morning it seemed more hopeful, forgivable. She hadn't cheated on him, after all. And she felt sure that everything that had passed between them meant that they wouldn't let this last thing—which she'd called a nail in the coffin but was really looking like a minor speedbump after a hellish collision course—keep them apart. But his phone only rang out. Was he training overnight on base? Was a family emergency to blame for his absence? She'd checked to make sure his phone wasn't blocked, so that wasn't it.

She made some phone calls, but since she wasn't family nor anyone his assistant knew or had registered under his emergency contacts, they couldn't reveal his whereabouts.

Though she was struggling to maintain her hopefulness by the time five o'clock rolled around, she marched directly to George's apartment to talk to him. She waited an hour and then decided to walk home. The wind wasn't very kind, but she needed to think.

About halfway home, Maggie saw a gallery with an open door, and it seemed to be calling her inside. It seemed like just the kind of diversion to give her a shift in perspective. Didn't artists spend all their time thinking about the kinds of heavy life questions Maggie was dealing with? On the other side of the door, it was cozy and warm, and she was handed a plastic cup of Chardonnay immediately. Now that was more like it.

The artist painted streets, cars, and traffic. Maggie was intrigued by her first look at canvas number one hung on its own perfectly white wall. An enormous gloomy scene that looked cold and normal, and depressing in its normality. *Was this what life was about?* it seemed to ask. She was often surprised at the art that pulled her in. How many hours had she spent trying to work out what it was that attracted her to a boxy wood cut of an ugly girl in front of a fireplace?

The path to the next painting took her past French doors opened to a surprising garden lush with wild greens and burnt-colored thistly natives, all of which she knew the names of still, all of which caused her to feel George around her. She had to trust that George would forgive her.

After that, Maggie was keen to see the rest of the works. The first had seemed to tap something inside her. And the tingle of sensation she got from the first painting led her to the anticipatory mood she was currently in the grips of.

The second painting was drenched in purple. A deep aubergine that made Maggie want to run out and get a wardrobe full of it. The subject wasn't so different from the first one, if you really looked. But it couldn't feel more dissimilar.

At first, she discerned only the angles—every few inches, the intensity of the purple would increase or decrease, and the sense of a rectangle would emerge, hard and edging out the colors and brush strokes around it. And another and another.

She took a step back to really grasp these "rectangles" as cars. Hundreds of them. Inside each was a unique microcosm. All evoked by the slight increase or decrease in color intensity. A softer swirl of the wrist was enough to create the sense of a family unit, a life, or a lack thereof, in each of those cars. Maggie could stare forever at a canvas like that, wondering how each collection of beings came to manifest that specific life, for that's what the cars represented to her. And she could choose which one she wanted. And she had. She'd chosen a car with George.

Maggie grimaced and let herself truly feel everything that was inside her. She knew it was all going to be okay. Some-where, she understood that even Flo would be okay. In one of those metaphorical "cars" Flo was driving along, living her own life. And despite all the untruths, they had truly loved each other. They'd served a purpose for each other. And in the end, Flo had helped Maggie get her life back on track. She wouldn't be here without her incredibly disturbing meddling.

And there was also a feeling trouncing on any bits of reason that emerged. And that feeling said, *you will miss her dearly.* Hopefully, in the end, they were both better for having known each other. Hopefully Flo could find her own happiness and leave everyone else to their own lives.

A man about her age came up behind her. "Why don't you bid on that painting? It's obviously got some kind of spell on you."

"I just might."

And she did. Two hours later, a slightly tipsy Maggie carried her new painting clumsily into her apartment, though the curator begged her to let them deliver it.

Years later, she'd come to see the painting as connected to Flo. She still thought of her. Love didn't die just because it was out of reach and the circumstances were not what they appeared to be. Feelings were real. The times they shared were real, and she wasn't going to let that be taken away.

Besides, she felt that Flo had taught her something, and sensed deeply that she had taught Flo something. In fact, the purple painting had come to grow a skin of their friendship over it, so that when she looked at the artist's take on life in all its permutations, she saw their shared history, and in one of those cars, a future for her and her friend who'd given her back the love of her life—concurrent, if not together.

One day, she'd think she'd seen Flo by the Manly Ferry Terminal. The woman would have Flo's hand gestures, her dense curls, and her lovely height. She'd have a man's hand on her *derriere* in a way that showed she was wanted. It wasn't Reg. Maybe she imagined it, she'd think. But she'd hope she hadn't. It was the best outcome she could wish for her friend.

THIRTY-SEVEN

MAGGIE

THE MORNING after Maggie leaned the purple painting over the mantle, her bell rang, but there was no one there. She ran down the steps and opened the front door. She looked left, then right. No one. She didn't recognize any of the cars out front either.

Out of the corner of her eye, she saw a bit of bright yellow. It was a Post-it Note stuck to her bell.

You have been invited to the Manly Ferry. There will be a ticket for you at the booth at noon.

She recognized George's handwriting. She tried not to think Flo had perfected forging it.

She showered and changed, took a long look at her painting over a nice cup of tea and smiled at the comfort it gave her.

She went to the booth, as directed. A ticket was in an envelope. The envelope said, *You have nothing to be sorry for. We're going to pick up where we left off, but I've got us a new destination. You might say it's bringing us full circle.*

Maggie smiled hugely. She walked over to the terminal and there he was, standing at the railing, the bridge and Opera

House in the distance. So much beauty. Everything was looking up.

"So why didn't you answer my texts?" she asked, diving right into his arms, delighting in the scent and feel of him.

"What text?" he said, his smile made it to his eyes.

"Not again!"

"Just kidding," he said.

She slugged his arm.

"Too soon?"

She smiled. They fell into a huge, cathartic laugh, which ended in him pulling her close. God, he smelled good. His hair was still wet and that made her think of him in the shower, which made her think, oh—where was she? "So why didn't you answer?"

"I wanted to show you how I was going to make things right, instead of telling you."

"Hmmm, what are you going to show me?"

"You'll see." He took her hand and led her over the bridge to the ferry, which had just secured its anchor. "After all these 'you show me yours' innuendos, I've dreamed up a lot of scenarios." He sat her in the same seat where they'd taken that photo once upon a time.

"Why don't you tell me about them?"

"Well, the first one starts like this." George leaned in, cupped the back of her head in his hand and pulled her close. Her eyes closed to savor the moment. The anticipation of his lips making contact with hers mingled with the excitement of their whole lives ahead of them.

She waited, but when nothing happened, she closed the distance between them. Fire ripped through her. She pressed harder than she'd intended, but even that wasn't enough. He appeared to experience the same urgency, pulling her into his arms. His erection grazed her leg and created tremors where it made contact with her heat through her skirt.

They both realized they were getting carried away and she pulled her lips from his, rested her head on his shoulder. He pulled her in close, his arms tight around her. God, this was perfection.

The ride was smooth, the odd spray cool on her bare legs. When they disembarked, she was taken back again to that first week in Australia, to their perfect beginning. Only it was more perfect now.

They walked the shore, each spot springing memories and sensations—now, finally, without pain, and instead, enriching each step toward their future.

"We're here," he said, halfway down a beachfront block.

"You rented this place again?" It was the beautiful cottage they'd stayed all those years ago.

"Nope." He smirked.

She cocked her head. "So what's going on?"

"We bought it."

"We did?" Her smile was overwhelming.

They began kissing fiercely, trying, she guessed, to shed their individual existences to create this new joined one. "Oh, George! I'm so happy!"

"I know. I'm just as happy. Come on," he said, dangling the keys. "Let's go have a look."

As he led her through all the rooms, the feeling of joy, of coming full circle, overwhelmed her.

"And my favorite room," he said, "the bedroom."

Inside was an air mattress and two small side tables. One look at the bed and she jumped into George's arms. Their bodies said what their words hadn't been able to all this torturous time.

"Oh, Maggie. Oh, Maggie. Oh-" the words seemed to come

without him consciously saying them. A mantra. It made her fire for him burn hotter.

"I want you, George. Please, make me yours. Take me to that place. I need to be in that place."

"Yes," he said. "Oh, Maggie—"

She yanked at his buttons. Each further revelation of skin brought moans to her lips. She had to put her mouth there. And there, and there.

As she did, he brushed the hair from her ear and kissed her all down her neck, his tongue lashings reverberating through her body in sync with her mouth on him. Pure instinct. No wonder she couldn't let him go despite the guilt she'd felt.

He took her hand and stood her before him. His fingers teased at the slim strap of her dress, then dipped down, sending sparks through her body. He let one slip over her shoulder, then the other. He turned Maggie around, slowly lowering the zipper in back until she was standing in nothing but her black lace thong.

"Oh my God, look at you. You forgot your bra."

"I didn't. I was thinking of you. I was feeling naughty and a little dirty. I decided to skip it."

"Why the thong then?"

"I know you like them."

"Oh, you're right about that," he said as he pushed against her. She gasped. He kissed her neck as she rocked against his hardness.

She turned and undid the buttons of his jeans to reveal black boxer briefs.

"And if I recall, you have a thing for these boxer briefs too."

"Oh shit."

She fell into him, their kisses ferocious, teeth and shallow, desperate breaths. He lifted her to him, her legs wrapping around his waist.

"Enough waiting," he said.

He carried Maggie to the makeshift bed, kissing her all the while, and in one swift movement, lowered her, removed the material of his underwear between them, and tugged her tiny panties aside so his tip made contact with her hot wetness.

"Oh God," she said as he teased her, his groaning showing Maggie he wouldn't be able to wait much longer. In this moment, she didn't know how they'd managed to make it this long. There should be some kind of medal awarded.

She lifted her hips to hurry him along, to satiate her desire. But he resisted, sliding the tip out slightly to ease the delicious pressure at her opening. Only for a second. And then he plunged in.

Their moans joined. Their bodies pushing and his hands gripping her tighter, then even tighter to him. This. Oh. She feared what this would do to her if things ever ended between them. As he brought her closer, it was toward a kind of death. Because independence was a thing of the past. This was the real, dangerous thing. Love.

She groaned as his thrusts were too much and her body pulsated around him. "I love you," she yelled, giving herself over to him completely, in the tidal wave of sensation.

"Say it again," he said.

"I love you. I love you."

And he slid out and came in an explosion on her thighs, then pulled her in to his chest like he would never let her go.

She slid her fingers around the wetness, amazed at how quickly she fell back into the animalistic hunger for everything George she'd always sweetly suffered from.

He seemed to read her mind. "Don't be afraid," he said. "I love you." He gripped her fingers, wet from their sex, and gazed into her eyes. "Marry me. Marry me, now."

"Aren't you gonna ask my dad first?"

"Already did," he said.

"You did? Presumptuous, don't you think?"

"Well, then you're really going to think my next revelation's presumptuous."

"What have you done?"

"Got your dad and Jessica on a plane here. They land in two hours."

"Bet you've planned the wedding too?"

"Yup. It's here at our new house." He walked her to the window. There were ocean views as far as the eye could see.

"I know it's a bit of a wreck at the moment, but I'm going to work on that. In fact, that's going to be my new career. You know I learned the building trade from Dad. Made him pretty rich, but more than that, it's honest, hard work right here where you are, which is what I want."

"Aren't you manly?"

"You have to ask?"

She smiled and kissed him tenderly.

"So, will you marry me?"

That started them up again.

In the shower, he soaped her up where he'd been fucking her, gently rolling his fingers through her folds, driving her crazy again.

"Stop." The word didn't carry the weight it needed for him to actually stop. It was delicious and quick the way he kissed her and touched her there, reacquainting himself with every bit of her, sucking and lingering like he was satisfying a hunger he'd suffered too long.

When he brought her to climax and then rested his head in the crook of her waist, the water raining pleasantly over them, she continued the conversation they'd begun before round two.

"Let me get the details before I wind up at my own wedding without even knowing where it is."

"It's in Coogee. On the beach. At our favorite spot."

"Oh, George." She brought her hand to his shaft and grasped around the base.

"I thought you wanted to know all the details."

"Never mind. Sometimes surprise is good. Now come here," she said, kneeling, bringing him—and because of his pleasure, her too—to ecstasy. Round three.

"Why, Mr. Hendricks, I do declare!" She did her best Scarlett.

"I know, it's ridiculous."

"No. It's wonderful. Because I know it's true. Which is why I'm never going to let another woman near you again."

"Well, then you're going to have to make this official."

"If I *have* to."

He smiled and pulled her into his chest as close as two people could get. "You do," she said.

He reached behind her, and she heard a drawer slide open.

"Are you going through my drawers?"

"Thought we just did that."

"Ha ha—oh!" He gently placed a black velvet box on the pillow between them, then gazed into her eyes. Oh, that smile. She forgot how incredible that smile was. . . the one she'd only seen him give to her.

George hinged the lid open to reveal a stunning, perfectly round diamond in a gold setting. He'd remembered she always wore yellow gold. It was exactly what she would have chosen for herself.

"Let's make this official. Will you marry me, Maggie?"

"Yes! Yes! A million times, yes! I'm never letting you go again. Except next week, of course."

"What do you mean? I'm not going on deployment. I'm leaving the Army."

"If you want me to marry you, then you will. You go to Iraq.

You want to do this. You need to do this. If you still want to leave, we can revisit that when you get back."

He began to protest, and Maggie put a finger to his mouth.

"Don't say it, George."

"Hear me out," he said.

She dipped her chin.

"I will not leave you. Ever. And this means I am leaving the army."

She opened her mouth to argue.

"Wait. I know what you're going to say. And you're right. I don't *have to,* but if I really want things to work with us—forever work with us—then I do. You didn't mean to pull away when I left for Afghanistan all those years ago. But you did. And I did too. It's not the right thing for us now. And this isn't the last time we'll be apart if I stay in. It certainly won't be the last time we relocate. And I don't want that for us. I want a life with you. Here. A forever life."

THIRTY-EIGHT

GEORGE

SHE UNDERSTOOD the weight of my decision to leave the army. I could see her reassessing the facts of the case in light of this new information. I wasn't fucking around. "And the truth is, I'm scared shitless about what my life will be like after the army. So scared, I haven't been able to take one step toward that new life. As far as everyone knows, I'm off to Iraq in two weeks."

"If leaving the army is what you really want to do, then I will support you. But right now, I know you need to go to Iraq, stay the course."

"After everything I just told you, how can you say that?"

"Because I know you. And you aren't a person who procrastinates. You're a person who files the paperwork and then gets on the plane. I know you're afraid because of our past, but we are not those people anymore."

"You *want* me to go?"

She let out a huge sigh and I saw her grow taller and look more confident and beautiful than I'd seen her in a long time. "No. I *need* you to go. I've gone through all the scenarios so many times. What I know is that I want to be with you. And I know you want to be with me.

"No matter where you go now, I know you and I are forever. There's nothing we can do to stop it. But we can do it properly. And I don't think you're ready. You need to go to Iraq, finish what you started. I will be here when you get back, in our beautiful home. There is nothing that can keep us apart now. You have been so thoughtful in considering my needs, and now it's your turn. This is a two-way street. I love you and I want you to do this."

"I love you so much, Maggie. You're amazing. And you know what they say about absence making the heart grow fonder."

"Do I *know?* I could have written the book on it."

"And after this morning, you could have written the book on what it should look like when all that fondness is finally unleashed. Again."

"You can write a pretty hot book about that yourself. And just for the record, I'm considering a few different scenarios for that book. This was just scenario number one." I pulled the ring from its slot and reached for her hand, slipped it on. It fit so perfectly, like it was made for her. I held it away to look at it, then drew her to me and kissed her.

My mouth lingered, I rubbed her hand on my cheek, like she was a part of me now and I wanted her to know that. I decided to say that out loud. Oh my, scenario number two got incredibly hot after that.

We lay like that until it was time to pick up her dad and Jessica, savoring the feel of being together, re-learning, and finally giving into, what it felt like to be so loved.

"YOU GONNA SHOW me how the third scenario starts now?" Maggie asked when they were once again lying together later that evening, a brilliant night sky outside the window of their new Coogee home. A couple of stars twinkled, framed by the pane, like they'd been placed there just for the benefit of these lovers. There wasn't a lick of furniture in the house. Just this air mattress and dozens of candles George had lit around them.

They'd announced the good news to her father and step-mother at dinner. Her father had been so happy. "Your mother would love George," he said. Jessica nodded. God, for someone who'd made so many mistakes with the people she loved, she'd certainly turned out lucky in the end. And she knew it was because she'd made her own luck—looked her fears in the eye and forged ahead to George anyway. And he'd done the same. Strong as he was, it was difficult to consider his weaknesses—but she had a lifetime ahead with him to get good at that.

"Of course. Then the fourth, and the fifth, all the way until I get on that plane to Iraq."

"Let's not talk about that right now."

But it was there with them, the reality of the brevity of their time together, of all the risks both known and unknown when he was over there. It lent fire and a sweet pain to their lovemaking.

There would always be elements she couldn't control. There would always be the possibility of being burned, but if she didn't give herself over to the rewards on the other end of those risks, then she'd never really live. And this, she was one hundred percent certain, was exactly what living looked like. And she'd risk everything for it.

DEAR MAGGIE,

I just wanted you to know I have been in a relationship with a woman after the strange fling with Flo (she cut her hair like yours, by the way). I thought you might contact me to ask for the statue I gave you on our first anniversary, as it was mistakenly put in one of my cartons, but you didn't.

Now I want to tell you that Lianne is pregnant and we are going to get married. I rather love her. She doesn't mind my absent-mindedness (yes, I know I am), and she has incredibly loving ways of reminding me to do the things I need to. She cares in a way you didn't.

I'm sure this will come as quite a surprise to you.

But maybe it won't. I do, though, hope you are as happy as Lianne and I are.

Sincerely,

Reg

PS: Here is a photo of me and Lianne at our engagement 'do. So you can see, I am completely over you.

WHILE I WAS IN IRAQ, Maggie and I kept things interesting in some naughty ways that I am surprised I didn't get court marshalled for.

I hired a contractor, a guy I knew from school, who'd let me work alongside him when I came back. He laid tile, poured concrete, knocked down walls, installed windows that Maggie picked out to make our house into the home she wanted to share our future in. She emailed me photos of everything. I felt she was beside me the whole time, the way I always did. But even more intensely.

And I knew that despite the missteps, the collateral damage, the ugliness of the final kaboom that was the Flo breakup, we had made it. This was the kind of love worth fighting for. And I'd spent my whole lifetime learning how to fight. I was excellent at it and I was not going to lose this battle.

THE END

Here's your next hot read from the Flame Series: Will Lachlan get a happy ending of his own?

Start reading the first chapter now!

CHAPTER 1
SCARLETT

WHEN THE ALARM went off it shocked me. Heart pounding, breath caught in throat, jolt to the limbs shock. I barreled through the emotional rapids until I realized it was morning. That dream was incredible. So incredible, I squeezed my eyes so I wouldn't leave it behind just yet. After two more cycles of that torturous iPhone tone, with its cruel quietening at the end of each riff, I pressed snooze.

I've always had a ridiculously vivid dream life, but lately they've been x-rated, which was new. There he was—again. That faceless man. I never did get close enough, though I could feel my fingers twitching to touch. It was a delicious torture, night after night. But it was fair. I wasn't letting any man close enough to hurt this precious family again and Dream Me understood that and played along. In an increasingly dirty girl way.

I opened my eyes long enough to hit snooze and squeezed my lids shut again, telling myself that today I'd permit a few extra minutes of exquisite eroticsm with Mr. Faceless, Whose Face I Knew By Heart. My subconscious mind was being cheeky, but all that did was make me more desperate to conjure up his chiseled cheekbones, the look of his hand scrubbing at his hair, and that downward tug of his brow. I've studied that seductive gaze of his many mornings in the real world. But in the real world, women like me—who've been knocked up and left to raise a child on her own—don't find naughty situations alluring. They find them costly.

But that's what dreams are for. In my mind's eye, I tried to place him across from me, at the door of the train. Strangers all around. There was the smell of vinyl seats and brake oil. There was his commanding stance, chest open, elbows out, taking up space unapologetically. Of course he was being noticed.

I still couldn't see his face but oh, I had only the one I imagined on him. I wasn't fooling myself even if I kept trying to. It was the guy from the train, which is why the dream cunningly disguised our meeting *on the train*—where I saw him in real life every day, until about a month ago. Now, in my bed, clearly desperate for a taste of the glad eye he always had for me, I conjured him inching toward me, a mutual awareness of each other weighing down the air around us. He was turning, painfully slowly. But then—

I forced my eyes open. That was enough of that. I jabbed at the phone screen and saw I'd given myself an extra fifty-two seconds. A record for straying from my responsibilities. Even that brought on a twinge of guilt. I turned and saw my little girl. Zooey looked so angelic, her little nose just inches from mine, tufts of her springy, pale curls radiating around her like a halo. At three and a half years old, she definitely had her no-good father's blue eyes and a lot of his other features, which meant I had to think about him a lot more than I wanted to think of the man who'd left my daughter fatherless. Still, at moments like these, her downy glowing at her cheekbone in the morning light, I couldn't help but think how lucky I was to have such a wonderful girl who brought so much love and life into the world.

It was just the two of us—Zooey and I—since my sister had moved on and found a place of her own a few blocks away. To fill the gap and assure all of us I could and would nail this single mom thing on my own, I had gone all mother-hen and made this place beautiful and cozy, trawling second-hand furniture shops and every clearance bin at Target until it looked like a place featured in the catalogs my employer produced. I'd done well enough with the nest that she slept like a log here. A splayed out, blanket-stealing, jujitzu-kicking log.

But for most of the evenings this past week she'd been up all night. Someone had begun construction on the empty loft above us that used to be occupied on occasion by our landlord, Richard, and this was the fourth night in a row we'd been woken by screaming saws, nail gun shots, and drilling. Now I'm sure there are laws about stuff like that, but our lovely landlord— who'd become a friend over the years—had let us live in this apartment for well below fifty percent of market value for the past three years. I must have had a bit of secondary mourning from my own parents when he died earlier this year because I was so inexplicably sad about it; couldn't shake the hollow feeling. In fact, I was surprised lately by how many times a day he came into my thoughts.

In the practical sense, so far, whoever's taken over the reigns for him hasn't checked that Kath doesn't live here anymore despite her status on the lease. There's no doubt any other landlord would not be so benevolent. And without her salary there's no way we'd qualify for this place, so I was scared to rock the boat.

I was pregnant when Richard rented it to us. It's the only home my daughter's ever known. And don't I know there is plenty of chaos coming up in her life: like working out she's got a deadbeat dad who wants no part of us. So the least I could do, I've always thought, is to give her the comfort and continuity of a wonderful home. There, I hoped, was something I could control. I spied the space around us and felt more than ever how important this was for her. She smiled and sighed in her sleep as if underlining the point in the blissful quiet of the morning— only San Francisco's waking noises of birds and the odd car to be heard.

As far as I knew, no one else has lived up there since Richard. We occupied the first floor and there was his duplex above us, which Richard used to use every once in a while. Though he wasn't a constant presence in our lives, I missed him sorely. I know he was keen on Zooey from the way he fussed over her and brought her inexplicably extravagant gifts for no reason at all. We'd had plenty of dinners together down here on the other side of this wall, laughing and playing games like Guess Which Animal I Am. (Zooey is *always* a cat.) He was a lovely man, and I didn't think he had any family, and the way I saw it we instinctively understood each other as a result.

Though we didn't talk about any of that, he had a silent way of showing what we meant to him.

We never did telephone calls; it had always been a face-to-face when he was around kind of thing, but I always felt his care for us in his absence, and I sensed he felt ours. But whether he was there or not, there'd been blissful silence all the way through.

And now suddenly, here we were: racket, drilling, nail guns, whining saws, hammering. And me afraid to make waves. Still, I didn't know how much of this we could take.

Banking pillows around her on all sides, I let Zooey sleep for a little bit longer so I could have a shower. She had her third birthday four months ago, but old habits die hard. She was everything to me and I would make sure she was safe, no matter what.

Ten minutes later I was freshly showered with brushed teeth and styled hair. I'd just cut layers into the long dark waves and was still getting used to it. Today, I pulled both sides back the way the stylist had suggested, and this left my neck exposed, my cheekbones and eyes popping in a way they hadn't before. If I had a mind to think that way, I'd say I looked quite sultry.

I found my style of dress had changed slightly to go along with the new look and feel of the styled hair—more streamlined, tailored jackets, dresses and skirts. Who knew long plain hair had actually been making me feel and act plain? Amazing. But I was enjoying the new look and the refreshed energy it gave me. Let's face it: I'd had that tired mom thing going before. There were more ponytail days than anything else. And now I was beginning to remember what makeup could do, and the way that deep lipstick hues had brought out a sparkle in me. It had been a long time since I'd sparkled. Since I'd even thought to sparkle.

A glance at my deep, nearly red lip, and I knew there was no denying it: I felt bolder than the ponytail version of me. What's that saying? Change is as good as a holiday?

I made my way back to the bed and touched my nose right up to Zooey's. Her head smells like heaven. An indescribable freshness that makes me giddy. After a brief delay, her long lashes fluttered. It was love at first sight with her every day when her eyes opened and she smiled at me, her gums and tiny teeth on full display.

"Momma." God I loved hearing her say that. She reached out her little starfish fingers, blinking. I kissed her smooth little face repeatedly, until she shrieked in laughter, then did it a bit more. The room brightened suddenly--the sun flexing just for us in this gorgeous moment.

Zooey reached for Kitty, the battered, plush Tabby she clutched to her whenever she was home. We didn't take him to daycare because a loss would be disastrous, but that didn't stop a daily entreaty for *just this once!*

On cue she asked anyway, as she gave Kitty a good inspection eye to eye.

"Nope. We don't want to lose him; you know that. But we need to hurry up if we're going to get there on time."

Zooey didn't even pout. She only asked out of routine and never expected permission. She tucked Kitty under her arm, kicked the blankets off dramatically, then stopped suddenly to make way for a loud, exaggerated yawn that took up her entire little face and jostled her corkscrew curls. Then she shook it off, flicking me a smile that made her liquid blue eyes sparkle. God, I loved that kid.

I LOVE the work I do—production for a homewares catalog everyone is so familiar with it's been featured in sitcoms, and there's barely an American who doesn't have at least one piece from them, or a knock-off of one, in their home. But it's not work I thought about on the train ride today, as I take my regular seat. It was that man from my dreams.

It's no wonder I dreamt of him. Since the day he stepped onto my train car, we locked eyes with the kind of force this rail system wishes it could harness. Every day since—for nearly a year now—it's twenty minutes of white hot unspoken passion as we pass through San Francisco.

He stands directly in my sight line, looking so sexy in his modern cut European suits, his muscles bulging, his hand rubbing at his hair, igniting explosions beneath my skin. We gaze at each other with a lust so palpable I feel like everyone can see, and I don't even care. Every inch of my body goes on alert. It's absolutely insane. And I look forward to it each and every day. In fact, the afterglow of our exchange keeps me fueled all day on an erotic charge unlike anything I've experienced before. I've become an addict. I wouldn't dare tell a soul how attached I'd become to a perfect stranger. Or worse, that it feels like he isn't a stranger at all.

But I was cut off at the source when a couple of weeks ago he abruptly stopped showing up. I've had to train myself not to expect his return because it's such a crush when he doesn't materialize.

But that was a half-hearted attempt, whether or not I admitted it, because my eyes instinctively darted to "his" door at "his" stop, and when he didn't step on and the train pulled away, a massive emptiness shot into my chest. I told myself I was being stupid all day when I felt my energy depleted, or that the world had dimmed. *You don't even know his name.* But logic is not my friend with this one. Because if it was, it would say: *And you're not letting anyone in anyway, not with Zooey's happiness at stake.* But that's the great thing about fantasies. You can give in when you feel like it, and logic can take a hike without risking anyone's wellbeing.

There was an older woman who often occupied the seat beside me, and she was there this morning, and as always she kindly scooched back, pausing her pencil over her Soduku, to let me through to the window seat.

"Good morning Dear," she said. "Looking very trim. I like the haircut, too."

I hoped my smile didn't give away how deeply that compliment struck me. "Thank you," I said, my head dipping with the weight of sincerity. There were some very good people in the world. That's what I should have been thinking about. But as soon as my bag was settled on my lap, my gaze was settled expectantly at Mr Faceless' usual space. Flashes of my dream came to me in a wave of heat. I switched the cross of my legs just because I needed to do something with my body.

My figure was finally back in fighting shape. I wasn't one of those who bounced right back after the baby, and it was interesting how your relationship with your body could shift so many times in just a few years. When I was pregnant, people bypassed the usual boundary of personal space, their hands at your belly, their stares and well-meaning seat sacrifices defining where you stood in the world. Which was complicated in my case since Greg had taken off. I mostly felt like damaged goods with a blaring sign advertising the fact. And then Zooey was born and it was leaky, swollen breasts and flabby skin I thought of exercising but didn't.

Then, slowly, we got into a rhythm, and long walks gave way to long runs up and down San Fran's killer hills, and then Moms and Bubs yoga, and now fitness has continued to be a part of our lives. In fact I don't know how I would have survived without its endorphine rush, its powerful zen. Today, I was in my best shape ever. And our tiny family was doing well. The world was good. But my libido was screaming to be heard. *He isn't coming.*

The train shrieked along its track toward San Leandro, a place I had once been convinced was too far out of the center of town, but had become a peaceful, leafy enclave I was happy to commute to. *Especially since Mr Faceless came on the scene.*

I looked out to the door where I'd seen him enter so many times. Would he be back today? My chest rose with the possibility as we approached Orinda, his stop.

Was I carried away with this stranger? You bet. But when you've got a two-year-old and you're on your own just trying to make ends meet, it's a pretty nice distraction. The train slowed, the stop was announced. My eyes scanned the crowd on the platform.

The doors opened. My breath went shallow. My octogenarian neighbor looked my way. My reaction to him—when I hadn't even seen him yet—was so intense, I would be surprised if people couldn't tell.

There was the usual crew—students with their bulky backpacks and buzzing headphones, the tech guys you can pick out from their disheveled looks, the glossy female executives. But no Mr. Faceless. I can't explain how upset I was when the doors closed with no sight of him. Rationally I understood I didn't even know him, and yet it didn't register that way. I get it, you always want what you can't have. And silly as that sounds, it was true, I felt my desire for him build. I wouldn't be surprised if I burst into flames.

In twelve minutes I had reached San Leandro, and then I was at my building: elevator, coffee, small talk, a quick meeting in the conference room, dozens of emails. Then I spent the better part of the day dealing with a third-rate model who clearly had herself confused with Kendall Jenner, if her demands for a certain brand of sparkling water were any clue.

Usually it's a pleasure to help make this catalog, dealing with creatives who can style a look and feel that makes life that little bit more enjoyable. As a producer, I bring all the experts together, and that also means I'm the one to get yelled at when it all falls apart, which is fair enough. I like the responsibility, which is something I learned being a mom. In fact, the more the better. It makes me feel grounded, needed, purposeful. Which wasn't enough to fan away the flames of desire that dream and this morning's expectant train-ride had ignited.

I would have thought that would have been the perfect recipe for more dirty dreams.

Nup. But that's only because the building racket had started before we even returned to the house that evening. The second time Zooey woke up, I decided to go upstairs to see what I could do without getting myself evicted. There was a whole team there. I could spot four guys. Clearly whoever had begun this project was in a rush to get it done.

"You know there are laws about these things," I said.

"Well, the boss said nobody was in the building and since it's retail spaces on either side nobody was here overnight, so it was okay to work through."

"Well, clearly there is somebody in here. As you can see. And that somebody has got a little girl downstairs who needs her sleep."

"I am sorry about that Ma'am. I've got a few of those myself at home so I understand where you're coming from, and I'm happy to have you take it up with the boss tomorrow. We can give you RAL's number."

"I've got the real estate company's details, thanks."

"But for tonight, we've got deadlines and if we don't hit 'em we don't get paid. And then I can't feed my little ones. So we're going to have to continue."

"Wonderful. Sounds like the new boss is disgustingly ill-informed."

Back in my bed, Zooey nodding off in my arms on the couch, I tried to stay calm with my voicemail message, but that isn't how it came out. "This is the tenant below you at 23 Smith Street. I have a three-year-old daughter and she hasn't been able to sleep since you started this illegally timed construction. Can you please ring me and discuss a reasonable schedule?" The second I hung up, I regretted my words and the shrill tone they had been delivered in. What if we got kicked out?

Everything will be fine, I told myself. It was a reasonable request and it will be handled reasonably. Why should I expect the worst?

But after a very, very long, loud night, during which neither Zooey nor myself got more than ten minutes of sleep at once, I still hadn't gotten a call back from RAL Real Estate. I left another message this time promising myself I'd be composed.

"Hello. I'm the single young mother whom you ignored last night." *Great start!* I held the phone up so he could hear the drilling. "I'd hoped to hear from you by now, but I haven't. And after another night of no sleep you need to stop the evening work immediately or I'm going to the police." I hadn't meant to go there. Why would I want to put the idea of getting anyone in trouble into anyone's head? While I'd come across slightly more assertive, I'd definitely taken it to a new level.

I didn't really want to go to the police. Zooey cried when I woke her, and I can't say I blamed her. It's widely known that lack of sleep is a method of torture. I went through the morning run drop-off chaos, then ran for the train. I slid in past my regular senior neighbor, got myself sorted, and told myself I would *not* expect him today.

But I was already conditioned. It felt good to look at the space he'd often occupied and conjure up that elicit look we shared, cleansing. I breathed out the anger and breathed in the lust. And the lust was better.

I was not anticipating, I told myself. I was *meditating*. I was in my happy place. This was healthy. As the commuters poured through the door on the stop before Mr. Faceless's, there was a part of my brain that said I really needed to get a life—*imaginary romances with strangers who weren't even here!*

The doors shut and the train careened toward the next stop. I wouldn't even look. I didn't need to. I had self control. He wasn't going to be there anyway. I kept my gaze trained out the window at the queue slowly shuffling aboard. There were the same tech guys and glossy women. I also spotted cardigan guy, punk nose ring girl, non-punk nose ring girl, basketball boy, and a couple dozen corporate clad executives. My eyes scanned through them all one by one—until, bam!—There. He. Was. And was I freaking crazier than I thought a minute ago, or did he just flash me the sexiest smile?

In case I took too long to consider it, he dipped his chin once. Just to check, I smiled back. His grin stretched to epic proportions. I pinched myself in what I hoped was a discreet way to make sure I wasn't having another one of my lurid dreams. It fucking stung. This. Was. Happening.

And suddenly, he was parting the sea of people and seating himself diagonally across from me. My senior friend turned purple, grinned maniacally, then swallowed a giggle. Now I wanted to pinch *her*.

I hadn't been embellishing. He looked amazing. He was in a black suit and boy did he fill it out nicely. I tried not to gawk as I took in his biceps and shoulders, the way his tie lay over his ridiculous pecs. This was so a dream. For one, he never sat near me. What we did was across a crowded car. There was no making it real. It had nothing to do with real.

"Hello," he said. It occurred to me I'd never imagined his

voice. If I had, I could not have outdone this: He. Had. An. Australian. Accent. *Fuck me.* I wouldn't call myself shallow, but I would call myself weak. And the way that velvety word came out of his mouth made me weak*er*.

"Hello." I pretended Senior Citizen Lady wasn't darting her gaze back and forth, like she was watching tennis instead of being unashamedly nosy. My face burned.

I had never been that close to him before. My skin felt electrified. I became hyperaware of all the bits of us and where they were in proximity to each other. I felt myself flush. Would we really keep going this way or would one of us talk again? Just being near him changed everything. The air felt different. I swore I could actually feel it against my skin. The sun shined in through the window. Senior Citizen Lady felt like a friend I was sorry to have mentally insulted, and I realized *I* was the jerk: why didn't I know her name after three and a half years?

Thank god I didn't do letting men in or I might be under the ridiculous understanding that this was love at first sight. What else could this feeling of intense nausea, desire, and elation so huge it could lift the world be? Jesus Christ I had missed him. I felt a lump form in my throat. I breathed deeply a couple of times until I felt it pass.

He cocked his head, quirked a brow.

"What?" I asked, answering my own question about who would break the stalemate.

"Nothing," he said, flashing that megawatt smile again.

I was lit up like a Christmas tree even though I hadn't slept a wink. I was pumped with adrenaline and felt as out of control as a horny teenager alone with the boy she liked.

I opened my mouth to say, "It's good to see you," but thankfully he spoke just a second earlier.

"I haven't seen you in a while," he said.

Wow, what a way to say so much in so few words. And yeah,

it wasn't lost on me that the sentiment was the same as the words I was about to say.

"New dress?" he said.

"Yeah, I wore it while you were gone." Yup, that was my panties, melted. I knew the ground we were covering was immense for a first conversation. But it didn't feel like a first conversation. It felt like the relief of something I'd been desperately awaiting, finally coming to fruition. With the added bonus of incredible lust—a thing I'd gone without for so long I'd been imagining a romance with a stranger on a train. *This stranger on a train.*

"Now I feel like I missed out."

Our smiles mirrored each other's. It felt like physical evidence of how we perfectly fit—a match. I nearly forgot I didn't believe in any of that and that even if I did, I had a daughter who was priority number one. Men had no place in our lives thus far and that had felt safe and right. And aside from this little fantasy of mine, none of them struck me as worth upsetting the apple cart anyway. *And neither is this one,* I told myself. I actually laughed. Out loud.

His eyebrow lowered, but his smile had gone all the way to his eyes; the crinkles caused a jolt of white heat in places I'd not thought of in a while. He was amused. It felt like he knew what I was thinking about him. There was no recovering. The only way was to forge ahead.

"Where have you been?"

"I had to go back to Australia," he said.

I nodded.

"Did you miss me?"

Oh, that was the kind of devilish grin that could get a woman in some real trouble. Well, I wasn't going to answer *that.* I went for a dubious expression, scrunched eye and pouted lips.

"That means a lot, thanks. I read body language," he said.

I laughed out loud. Oh, and that did the most spectacular thing to the eye crinkles. *I* did that spectacular thing to the eye crinkles. Good doesn't begin to describe how I felt. I breathed in hugely, to calm the giggles, and that's when I was hit with the true weight of how insanely good he smelled. Ridiculously masculine—sage? Wood? A fresh, woodsy scent that made me feel like a horny sixteen year-old high on my crush's Cool Water. *Delirious.*

"I'm Lachlan," he said, and put his hand out. Why did putting a name to it increase the intensity a hundred-fold? Thank god I was sitting down.

I stared at it, while my throat dried up. I reached out and tried my best to say, "Scarlett."

When our palms made contact, tingles shot from the spot and jolted through my body. Every hair was standing on end. His fingers covered mine. I gulped as we both looked there.

"Wow," he said. A part of me was insecure, but that part was overpowered by the bit that knew exactly what he meant. When I'd heard him say *Lachlan,* I'd had the exact reaction.

"Impressed you didn't make any Rhett Butler jokes," I said.

"I've no interest in giving you more of the same."

Oh, my. Senior Citizen Lady (*Carrie? Ellen?*) buried her nose so close to her Sodoku I feared she'd get a paper cut.

"So what brings you on this train most days? Work?" I asked.

"Yup. You?"

"Same." It was very hard to speak when we were locked in this gaze. I swore I knew a lot of words. I just couldn't think of any of them. And yet, the gaze was saying something all its own and it certainly had nothing to do with the work I had so mundanely thought to ask about.

"What do you do?" he asked.

"Photo shoot production." It hit me that no one else on this train knew that. Not even Old Lady. Just another way I felt bonded to him.

"That sounds glamorous."

"Sure, it can be, but most of the time it's about anorexic models screaming about the type of bottled water we have on offer."

"Well, that's quite important, isn't it?" Never seen such an excellent deadpan. His only give was the slightest brow quirk.

I had lived my whole life up until then knowing nothing about Australia outside of what I'd garnered watching *Crocodile Dundee,* but suddenly it seemed like a gaping whole I needed to fill.

"And what do you do?" I asked.

For the slightest fraction of a second his face dropped. If I'd blinked I would have missed it.

"I'm in property development," he said.

Why did that sound sexy? Let's face it: he could have said, *toilet paper,* and it'd sound hot.

"I kind of fell into it."

"Do you enjoy it?"

"I think so." That struck me as uncharacteristically honest for a man in the position of having his first chat with a woman. Was it just me? Did he feel that pull of intimacy I did that overwhelmed normal behavior? Maybe I was making too big of a leap. Perhaps he was this way with everyone.

We studied each other for a second. My face heated.

"So can I take you out sometime?"

In my peripheral vision I saw Old Lady's grin peak out from the edges of her small book.

"Sure," I said. There was no point trying to hold back the smile. It was stronger than me.

If I could bottle this happiness, I'd save it for later, when he realized I had a three-year-old—the only other source I'd ever known of such pure happiness—and he went running for the hills.

He pulled out his mobile phone. "Can I grab your number?"

I gave him the number, he entered it, then tested it with a text message.

"Can I pick you up at 7:30 tonight and take you to Poesia?"

Weren't men meant to play games and drive you nuts? They certainly weren't meant to get right to the point like this. Perhaps after five months of visual foreplay, a little forthrightness is required. I was about to say, *I'll have to see if I can get a sitter*, but that would blow this up right now, wouldn't it? Boom. See ya. Could have been great.

"That's literally my favorite restaurant. Let me check my calendar," I said, buying time while I thought of a reason why he couldn't pick me up at my place. I couldn't think of one in time. I'd have to work it out later. "Okay," I said. "Sounds great."

The second the words were out, I regretted them. Dream men were not meant to cross over into reality. Everyone knew that. Especially me. I'd call my sister as soon as we parted ways to our respective offices, and she'd scold me and I'd call and tell him I made a mistake. I was a single mom and we just didn't do this sort of thing when we were awake.

Chapter 2
LACHLAN

THAT FIRST TIME seeing her since my return to San Francisco was *actually* like coming home. Funny, I'd been hunting down that feeling during my fortnight back in Australia and had only the slightest, fleeting glimpses of it.

Somewhere along the way I'd tried to convince myself the reality of her would not live up to the fantasy, especially the way

I kept poking at it as my tether to home base while I'd been back in Sydney these couple of weeks. But seeing her there on the train, with her new haircut, and that look that knocked me out, next to that same older woman pretending not to monitor our connection, and I knew it was all real, much as I was afraid to admit it. On the spot, I decided today was the day I was going to act on it. And the smile in her sultry gaze showed me she'd missed me too. That was all the reassurance I needed.

The normal spread of the pack into their usual spots, the handful of new people unsure of where to go, they all seemed to move in slow motion. But I savored every second because I'd been waiting for this moment.

My trip back home to Australia had been trying. Mum needed me. All the legal issues over my dad's death were making her anxious. And she didn't want to talk to Brian about them. She felt it was disrespectful since he'd been so good to us over the last ten years. And she was right. Brian was a stand-up guy. If she didn't have him, there was no way I would have taken off across the globe to take over my dad's business.

It was also easier to deal with the Aussie side of the legal and tax issues of my dad's death there, too. Having dual citizenship turns out to be a pain even in death. And there was the club opening, too. I'd invested in the nightclub when I first got wind of my inheritance as a final fuck-you to my dad. It was the kind of place that represented everything wrong in the world—showy, packed with influencers high on coke or fuck knows what else, where the most important thing was to fulfill every need of rich dickwads that didn't even tip properly. Now I was an ultra-rich dickwad; my opening move as one was to say, look, this is what your money symbolizes.

But I regret that now. You need to respect the dead. And living in their shoes gives you a wickedly unique perspective. Literally. Today I was wearing my dad's shoes. They were super expensive, and in excellent condition, and though I'd only put them on that first time during a very dark moment, it had felt, I don't know, almost religious—the connection it drew in my heart, the only connection I'd been able to conjure to him so far —and so, when I dressed most days, I found myself lacing them up. And the surprise result of that is you have no choice but to open your mind to any and all possibilities of why they fucked everything up so badly.

In fact, even on the night of the opening I already knew that was a real dick move. Which is why I got so stupidly drunk and let two girls have their way with me. Clancy, my oldest friend, was there with a girl he clearly had it bad for, and watching the connection between them had made me think immediately of the woman my inner voice inexplicably thought of as *My Girl*.

Now I walked my dad's shoes over and sat down across from her, in the open seat on a diagonal. The air felt different. I pulled at my cuffs to focus on something.

Just days ago I'd been as far away as you could get from San Fran, with two girls on either arm, and what had I been thinking about? *My Girl*. And now she was centimeters from me. In that dress. Holy fuck. I couldn't help from imagining the feel of my hands on her curves. The dress left little to the imagination. Could she have worn it for me? Nah, come on. I didn't even know her name.

One-click or visit your favorite bookseller to finish reading this steamy, slow-burn billionaire romance from the author behind the film Beauty & The Briefcase today!

For a free copy of Daniella Brodsky's novella, MY SIZZLING SECOND CHANCE, sign up for her readers' group. You'll get access to more free books, launch information, and lots more insider bonuses.

Daniella Brodsky is the Australian/American author of novels published by Penguin, Random House, and Simon & Schuster, most recently, *VIVIAN RISING* and most famously *DIARY OF A WORKING GIRL*, which was adapted for the screen by Disney, starring Hilary Duff. She also had a long career as a journalist and made a name for herself with *THE GIRL'S GUIDE TO NEW YORK* nightlife, back when she didn't need a babysitter and a disco nap to stay out past seven.

Daniella has taught fiction craft at the ANU, James Cook University. A native New Yorker, Daniella has lived in North Queensland, Canberra, Honolulu, Washington D.C., and Sydney; she teaches creative writing at James Cook University and at her Captain Cook Studio. If you're looking for domestic suspense, check out her pen name, Dan Noble.

www.daniellabrodsky.com.